Edited and designed by Pearce Marchbank
Text edited by Peter Hogan
Artwork and layout: David Fudger
Photographic printing: Adrian Ensor
Artwork assistant: Philip Levene
Typesetting: Lynne Shippam

Copyright © 1984 Gered Mankowitz
Introduction by Andrew Loog Oldham Copyright ©1984 The Living Group Trust
All rights reserved. No part of this book may be used or reproduced in any manner whatsoever without written permission except in the case of brief quotations embodied in critical articles or reviews.
For information, address St. Martin's Press, 175 Fifth Avenue, New York, N.Y. 10010.
Library of Congress Catalog Card Number 84-50987
First published in Great Britain by Sidgwick and Jackson Ltd.
First U.S. Edition

ISBN 0-312-69973-5

10 9 8 7 6 5 4 3 2 1
Printed in Spain by Editorial Elexpuru, S.A.L. Bilbao for St. Martin's Press, New York

Dedication: To Julia, for coming back.
Many thanks to: Peter Hogan, Pearce Marchbank, Adrian Ensor, Julian Hawkins, Caroline Lee, Eddie Read, Decca Records, Phil Levene and Dave Fudger.
Special thanks to Andrew Oldham.

WITH AN INTRODUCTION BY ANDREW LOOG OLDHAM

Satisfaction.
The Rolling Stones photographs of Gered Mankowitz.

St Martin's Press,
New York.

INTRODUCTION BY ANDREW LOOG OLDHAM

The Rolling Stones are a great fuckin' group, as true today as 20 years ago. The Stones, myself, Gered and the rest of the fortunate war babies of Britain who started their careers, with a partial compensation for World War II placing us at the center of the swinging sixties, when music, image and lifestyle collided and Great Britain orchestrated the rhythm of life, dressed, styled, informed and influenced the world with a passion that remains today.

In those days, fame for me meant always having your picture taken as you passed through airports. Film stars were the mold, Stars of Scandal became the alternative and rock and roll was the definition.

Like us and life, Gered was fast, had a passion for his work, took risks, could create images for all fields of our "commercial art", made a great cup of tea and met us in the right time at the right place with film in his camera and a famous father.

In the making of a record or a concert, the sound is either right or it kills you. A bad photographer can't kill you, except with boredom, but with the right photographer a group can explain and present themselves to the world in sound and vision.

When the camera and the subject fall in love, you can leave the room. With Gered Mankowitz I could always leave the room. I didn't often as I hate to miss a good show and with Gered there were many...

And here they are: Covers, Muvvers, Fans, Fags and Cigarettes
High Tide, Green Grass, Bit Hits and Between The Buttons
Out Of Our Heads (and you would have been too)
As Eddie rolled breakfast on Primrose Hill
And GM shot the Stones Between The Buttons and their sound in picture
December's Children and Everybody's
The taking of America (or did they take us)
Your sound is your sound, and your image makes it clearer
and if you sing the right song, Gered's number is...very good.

Thanks Lads. Thanks Gered. Thanks Life. See, Hear, Now.

Andrew Loog Oldham, New York, 1984.

SATISFACTION: THE ROLLING STONES BY GERED MANKOWITZ

"When I first photographed the Rolling Stones in April 1965, I was eighteen years old and beginning to establish myself as a successful photographer. I had my own studio, had gained a name for myself in the field of theatrical portraiture and had met and photographed several pop stars, including a young girl singer, Marianne Faithfull. Marianne's managers, Tony Calder and Andrew Loog Oldham, liked the pictures I'd taken of her, and one day I got a phone call from Andrew, asking me to do a session with the Stones.

"They came down to my studio in Masons Yard, just off Piccadilly, with Andrew, and we spent a whole afternoon trying various different set-ups, both in my studio, and on a building site just down the street. The session was phenomenally successful: in terms of usable material it resulted in album covers for *Out Of Our Heads* (*December's Children* in America) and the Andrew Oldham Orchestra's *The Rolling Stones Songbook*, plus a few publicity pictures, including one that would be used as the programme cover for their US tour that autumn. I don't think the Stones particularly enjoyed having their pictures taken, but they recognized that it was important, and once they'd committed themselves to a session, they threw themselves into it. One of the main reasons for that, I'm sure, was Andrew. He really was a powerful motivating force behind the Stones, and his being at the session that day was one of the reasons it worked — he could get everybody up and going; he really helped me to get them to respond to ideas. The other reason the session was successful was, I'm convinced, the fact that I was roughly the same age as them — a couple of years younger, but still a contemporary, somebody they could talk to and get on with. In those days, when the 'generation gap' was a very real thing, that was important.

"After that, I did a bit more work for Andrew — pictures of Marianne and one or two other artists, as well as work for other pop managers and some more theatrical stuff. Then late that summer — I'd just got back from holiday — I got a phone call from Tony Calder: 'How do you feel about going to America with the Stones?' I thought he was putting me on. In 1965, America was a lot further away than it is now — to be able to go there really was an adventure and a dream come true. And to travel with the Stones... You have to remember that the Stones were the second biggest group in the world, after the Beatles. In fact, to a lot of people, including me, they were even more important than the Beatles...far more spontaneous and exciting, and genuinely revolutionary. If the Stones were appearing on TV, you'd switch on *knowing* that they'd do something, or wear something that would cause offence to the 'straight' world. They simply breathed rebellion. So, when I realised the offer of touring with them was serious, I accepted like a shot.

"The theory was that every few days I'd send back some unprocessed film from wherever I was in the States to my studio in London, where it would be processed and proofed, and Andrew could then choose whatever shots he wanted to feed the media with. It was really one of Andrew's scams, to try and *build* interest — I don't think the press were that interested, beyond the fact that the Stones were big anyway...unless there were any major incidents. I had to agree not to photograph them at certain times, to allow them some privacy. When we had a few days break in the middle of the tour for a mini-holiday in Florida, Andrew said 'Don't take pictures. Treat this as a holiday'. It's a shame in a way, because whereas the Beatles were photographed doing absolutely everything imaginable, there wasn't that kind of attitude to publicity in the Stones' camp — maybe there wasn't the demand. Nobody *stopped* me taking pictures, but it was clear that they'd rather I didn't when they were 'off duty'. And unfortunately, nobody ever said 'Let's have some pictures of Mick and Keith songwriting in their hotel room' — which was a constant activity on tour; they wrote vast amounts of material, partly because there was nothing else to do. Because I'd been asked not to take photos in hotel rooms, there wasn't any material on that. I didn't push for it because it didn't occur to me then — and it was far more interesting for me to just sit back and listen.

"So we set off, one gloomy October morning, for America. We met in the VIP lounge at Heathrow airport — there were a lot of fans at the airport, so the Stones were hustled straight into the VIP lounge, then straight onto the plane. That was always a problem for the Stones — except out in the sticks, they couldn't go anywhere without attracting attention. Various wives and girlfriends came to say goodbye, and the atmosphere was a mixture of excitement and sorrow at leaving home.

"We were met in New York by Allen Klein, hustled through Customs and into a fleet of black Cadillac limousines — we managed to avoid the fan presence at the airport, but it was only a temporary respite. We were staying at a hotel on Broadway called the City Squire, which was a regular haunt for touring pop groups — I think Freddie and the Dreamers and Herman's Hermits were staying there at the same time. When we pulled up outside, all hell broke loose — there was an enormous crowd of little girls blocking the road. The cops were trying to hold them back, but at the same time trying not to injure them — they were banging on the sides of the car, climbing on the roof.... I think our driver was terrified in case anybody accidentally got injured. I'd certainly never seen anything like it, but the band took it all in their stride. In fact, even when the weight of the girls on the top of the car was causing the roof to buckle, so that Mick, Keith and I were literally holding the roof up with our hands, Bill was *still* trying to chat up the prettiest girls through the window. Finally, there was a break in the crowd, and the driver managed to get us in to the underground car park, the doors dropped shut behind us and we were away from it all. The security in the hotel was virtually airtight.

"The pattern for the tour established itself very quickly, even while we were using New York as a base and returning there each night. We had our own plane for the tour; a little two-engine Martin, with a pilot, a co-pilot and two stewardesses. Pretty basic, but even the band were excited about having a plane of their own. The first time we flew to a gig, Connie, the chief stewardess, was really concerned that we should have whatever we wanted for the tour — all we had to do was request our favourite food and drink, and they'd make sure it was on the plane. So while we were having tea, Mick said 'You know what would be really nice? Tea in china, with little lumps of sugar an' a teapot an' everythin', just like in England'...just teasing them, in a very mild way. By the time we flew back that night, they'd bought an English bone china tea service, and very proudly served Mick tea the way he wanted it.

"On the plane, besides myself and the Stones, were Bob Bowness, the tour manager (Andrew only joined the tour for short periods); support act the Vibrations, a black vocal group who carried their own supply of chili sauce so they could convert the standard airplane fare into 'soul food'; Patti Labelle and The Bluebells, who were the main support; a white American group called (I think) the Ramrods, who opened the show and also provided the backing for the Vibrations and Patti Labelle; Patti's manager, who used to be a boxing manager in Philadelphia; Ronnie Schneider, the tour accountant, who was Allen Klein's nephew and who was responsible for collecting the money from the promoters...and Ian 'Stew' Stewart, the sixth Rolling Stone. Stew had been fired from the group by Andrew, largely because his image didn't fit — also, I think six was considered too large a number for a group in those days. But Stew seemed to accept that, and he did look a bit incongruous next to the rest of them — he still looked like a teddy boy, and he was built a bit like Desperate Dan. He always carried a ton of stuff around in his back pockets, which tended to make his arse look enormous; he was always dead calm and sombre, and seemed quite happy to stay with the band as a roadie, taking care of all the equipment. When called upon, he still played the piano brilliantly. He was the only roadie, and I don't remember him even having any help in unloading the plane at each gig. I think a small transit van was laid on for each gig, and Stew would pile all the gear in that. It was all pretty basic — just four or five little Vox amps, which all the bands would use, and that was all. Occasionally Mick's vocals would be put through the PA system of the hall.

"Also on the plane was Jerry Brandt from the William Morris Agency, who'd booked the tour — his partner, Mike Gruber, was the advance man and usually travelled a day ahead of us. We'd also be joined quite frequently by Pete Bennett, the top record plugger in the States. 'Get Off My Cloud' was the current single, and Pete must have done a really good job on it — it went up the charts in exactly the way he said it would; if he said 'it'll be No 1 by next week', you believed him. And it *did* get to No 1 Pete also knew *everybody*, and could get you tickets for *anything*, and looked enough like a gangster in his shiny suit for Andrew to buy him a toy gun and shoulder holster. They then got into this comedy gangster routine — Pete following Andrew around saying 'Yes, Boss. No, Boss'. One time in Texas, Brian got moody on us. We'd stopped at a roadside burger joint for some food, and Brian decided to stay in the car; he wasn't hungry. So we had a meal, and were about to go back to the car just as Brian came *in* to the restaurant. We sat in the car for a while, and it became apparent that Brian intended to sit down and have a large meal, and everybody was pretty pissed off with him. Andrew turned round and said 'Go get him, Pete'. The restaurant was glass fronted, so we watched as Pete walked the length of the restaurant, picked Brian up by the scruff of the neck and frogmarched him back to the car, complete with half eaten hamburger. We were in hysterics; Brian was absolutely speechless. It wasn't untypical of Brian's stunts, unfortunately.

"The usual routine was a bizarre reversal of normal life. We'd get up at about four in the afternoon, have breakfast and then go to the gig. We'd arrive hours before anything was due to happen, to try and minimize the problems of getting past crowds of fans. As a result, there was always a lot of time to kill.

"The venues varied from small theatres to huge sporting arenas — the one in Chicago had been used a couple of days earlier for a rodeo, and the place still stank of horseshit. I'm convinced the dressing room had been used by horses. If the band were treated reasonably decently in that the hotels were bearable and the transport was well organized, the dressing rooms were definitely the other side of the coin. In a lot of cases the band were treated like absolute shit, so of course they took it out on their surroundings — they'd piss in the sinks and so on. Occasionally the local fan club would have been let in beforehand to decorate the place, so the walls would be covered in banners, poems, requests for songs and/or dedications, invitations to parties, presents, phone numbers... Several times there were birthday cakes — not that it was anybody's birthday, but it was a good excuse to try and get backstage — really ghastly Betty Crocker mix cakes, which usually ended up on the walls or in the loo. There were always interviews to be done, with local radio stations, TV stations, college papers...and there were always fans, somehow — friends of the security people... they'd get in by nepotism or bribery, whatever you did. Strangely, I don't recall the Stones ever being nasty to people, however much pressure they were under — they'd always take the time to sign autographs and talk to people.

"If the venue was a theatre, I'd often watch the support acts from the wings. The Vibrations were extraordinary — a curious mixture of Vaudeville and doo-wop. They'd just had a big hit with 'Peanut Butter' and like the Coasters, they were almost a comedy act — they had a fat soprano and a tall bassman, and a guy who would throw himself around. They'd inject slapstick into these really tight vocal routines. Patti Labelle and the Bluebells were magic. They did 'Somewhere Over The Rainbow', which was a real contrast to the Stones, to say the least, but it still went down bloody well. We actually ran into problems down South — gigs not selling out — through having black acts on the tour. I was shocked that the black acts weren't allowed to stay in the same hotels as us in certain Southern cities, and horrified whenever I encountered overt racism, but the more subtle signs of prejudice probably passed me by. It wasn't something I'd encountered in England.

"When the Stones came on stage, the screams would just be deafening. Even on a bad night, the excitement level was enormous — you can get a feeling of the audience reaction and atmosphere from the pictures. The police presence was always enormous, as was the security generally, but very unprofessional — kids would sometimes be thrown back bodily into the audience. Usually within the space of two songs, the first aid places backstage would be full of fainted and hysterical teenagers. Even though this sort of thing had been going on for years, since before Elvis I suppose, people were only just *beginning* to learn how to handle it, in that concerts now had security...the trouble was, the security had no idea how to deal with the audiences. As a result, often at the slightest disturbance the show was stopped, — in fact, in several towns it's a miracle the shows even happened at all, as the authorities came up with so many extra regulations at the last minute. Quite often the plug would, literally, be pulled on the band, the house lights would go up and the local sheriff would be on stage, trying to calm the kids down — 'You stay in your seats or else I'm going to stop the show'. Of course, when the plug went back in, Mick would start shaking his bum at the kids, teasing them and working them to fever pitch again. Not that Mick needed any encouragement, but I seem to recall Andrew egging him on on these occasions — Andrew being the man who used to pay teddy boys to slash seats at Little Richard concerts, I guess he felt that the ensuing publicity from these situations far outweighed any immediate damage. *Whatever* the show was like, Mick could always drive the audience bananas — he could lift

them, manipulate them any way he wanted.

"I suppose most of the material they were doing then was from *Out Of Our Heads* — it was the same set every night, though obviously the standard varied; some nights they were pretty awful, other nights they were absolutely magic. For me, 'Satisfaction' and 'Get Off My Cloud' were always the highspots — to this day I can't hear those songs without feeling the bass line running up my leg.

"The sound varied enormously. There were never any soundchecks as such — sound wasn't mixed in those days. If a guitarist had a bit of feedback, he just stepped back to the amp and adjusted it. No matter the size of the venue, every gig was like a club gig; all they had were five Vox amps. If it was a huge hall, all you could do was switch everything up to maximum and hope for the best. Sometimes the sound was great, when the acoustics and the balance were right. Otherwise, if you were on Brian's side you could hear Brian's licks, and if you were on Bill's side you could hear the bass... Most of it got drowned out by the screaming anyway. Those girls were *real* screamers.

"An endless stream of notes would be thrown onstage, often pinned to bras and underpants, with telephone numbers, quite lurid love poems and very explicit sexual offers, quite complicated messages, like 'Mom and Dad are away — ring me before eleven'... I was amazed by all this at first, but for the band, it was normal. I was continuously excited by the band, and by being on *stage* with the band. They didn't mind my being there at all — in fact, I think they quite liked the idea of having someone to record it. I was able to crisscross the stage, to get close up to Mick... I don't remember them ever getting annoyed with my presence. Everything was really basic — the lighting, everything. Whatever magic was there, was in the band's performance.

"During the last number I'd start to pack up my gear and get ready, because at the end of each show, before the audience even knew what had happened, we were all rushed out of the venue and thrown, sometimes literally, into limousines, and driven at breakneck speed to the airport. The rest of the entourage would already be on board, probably playing poker. We'd be airborne while the audience was still yelling for the encore.

"We'd arrive in the next town in the early hours of the morning, and be met by the local equivalent of a couple of limousines — extended checker cabs, or station wagons. The local radio station would be there, and invariably the local police chief...we sometimes got escorted with wailing sirens through totally deserted streets at three in the morning. Arriving at that time, the fan presence was minimal, which was partly the idea. Even so, the name of the hotel would often get leaked one way or another, and somebody would have to go into each room and flush out the fans. It wasn't at all rare to pull back the shower curtain and find two giggling fourteen year old girls. By far the majority of them would be sent home. Even if we got past that fan 'hurdle', by the time we got up the next afternoon the news had quite often got out — somebody on the night staff had talked. By then it didn't really matter — it was time for the next gig, then the next town.

"With few exceptions, I actually don't know where most of the photos on that tour were taken. With the kind of routine I've just described, it's not that surprising. None of us knew where we were half the time. I was woken up, put in a limousine, did my job, got on a plane and went to sleep in another town. It wasn't at all rare for conversations at breakfast to go along the lines of 'What town are we in? What day is it?' It was an absurd, gruelling routine, but it seemed to get the job done. There was always music around, though — in hotel rooms, on the plane...everywhere. There'd always be new records that somebody had discovered, or else there'd be jam sessions — Mick and Patti Labelle singing 'Somewhere Over The Rainbow', with Keith on guitar and the Vibrations doing doo-wop backing...great stuff. And Mick and Keith were writing the whole time; you'd hear odd lines and a bit of a tune and realise that it was a new song taking shape.

"There weren't really any groupies around in those days, except in New York and LA — certainly not the notorious kind that would come later, and girls like the Plaster Casters were unheard of. There were girls that would follow the band around — particularly Brian. They'd appear at concert after concert, travelling hundreds of miles between gigs, and almost certainly they stayed overnight at the hotel. I remember being slightly bemused as to how these girls persuaded people to drive them around the country. But they were camp followers, rather than part of the entourage.

"Truth to tell, there wasn't that much outrageous behaviour going on. There was some pot about, a little bit of speed, but that's about all. There wasn't even much heavy drinking. The bulk of the tour was just hard work, keeping weird hours... Mick and Keith got a lot of songwriting done, and of course people found ways of relieving the boredom, but it taught me that being a pop star is basically bloody hard work. It isolates you from reality, and tears you away from your loved ones. You accept the touring as something that you have to do, but when the travelling gets exhausting, even dangerous — I had a couple of nasty scares in our little plane and had no wish to wind up like Buddy Holly — and if the last concert was lousy, you ended up feeling pretty sorry for yourself. There was an unspoken rule that girlfriends weren't allowed on the road, and several of us got pretty homesick — I think Charlie was homesick even before we left Heathrow! I remember having a three hour conversation with Mick one night, both of us missing our girlfriends like hell.

"Of course, a lot of it was exciting, if only for me — it being my first trip to the States anyway, and there were plenty of ways to occupy the time. One hobby that we discovered on tour was 'mooning' — the art of baring your arse at an unsuspecting audience. There are numerous examples of that one, perhaps the most evocative being the time our two limousines were chasing each other — and being chased by a carload of fans — along an elevated motorway in Chicago. The cars were in radio contact with each other, living out a Highway Patrol fantasy, drawing level with each other then overtaking; at one point, as the cars drew level and our 'opposing' car pulled away from us, we saw Keith's arse framed in the car window, disappearing into the night.

"We met a fair number of celebrities: Andy Warhol, who was just a con-man with a great flair for publicity as far as I was concerned; and Bob Dylan, who I somehow expected to be a folkie in a denim jacket. Instead of which, I met a short guy in a blue mohair suit with a weird haircut. Dylan is reputed to have played at our hotel in New York on the night of the blackout, but if he did, I missed it. We were staying at the Lincoln Square Motor Inn by then, having been thrown out of the City Squire because of overzealous fan activity. The hotel was opposite what is now the Lincoln Square Center, which at that time was actually

SATISFACTION: THE ROLLING STONES BY GERED MANKOWITZ

being built, so we had a great view of the building site. Charlie and I had been out shopping, and were heading back when the lights went off — the whole East Coast was out for about nine hours. Within half and hour, all the bars were full of businessmen and their secretaries getting plastered, and within an hour, every hotel room in town was taken. By the time Charlie and I got back to the hotel, things were pretty well organised — they were handing out nightlights, with strict instructions that these should be placed in glass ashtrays, so as not to ruin their cruddy furniture. When we got to our floor, a party was already under way — the band all had these portable record players, which were battery operated, with the speakers in the lid...truly, the ghetto blasters of the day. Naturally, there were girls, booze and dope in abundance, and by one in the morning, we were totally wrecked. It was a great party, bouncing around from room to room by candlelight. What nobody realised about these nightlights, was that the wax got *hot* — so hot that it caused a glass ashtray in my room to shatter, sending a shower of wax onto my bed and setting it on fire. I remember Ronnie Schneider and I running into Bill's room for shelter, to be followed minutes later by a couple of smoke engrimed girls who'd put the fire out with water from ice buckets. When the lights came back on at five in the morning, there were grubby, half dressed people everywhere — on beds and under them. It wasn't an orgy at all — *you* try holding a nine hour party in the dark, and see that you look like. The next day the manager came to survey the wreckage — human and otherwise — in my room with a pert 'Is this where the fire was? I see. Have a nice day.'

"Once down South, Charlie and I were beaten up in a hotel coffee bar by a little old lady who looked exactly like Granny Clampett out of *The Beverly Hillbillies*. She'd taken a dislike to us because of the length of our hair, and proceeded to beat us round the heads with her umbrella. The manager was able to lead her away quite peacably in the end, but it demonstrates the way that people reacted to the 'younger generation' in those days — it was a different world.

"One of my fondest memories of the trip came right at the end of the tour, after the last gig in LA. Before the band went into the recording studio, Keith, Ronnie Schneider and I disappeared for a few days riding holiday in Phoenix, Arizona. Keith invited us, and paid all our expenses, which was really sweet of him — frankly, we couldn't have afforded it otherwise. The first thing we did — at Keith's insistence — was to get kitted out from top to bottom in cowboy gear...ten gallon hats, chaps, everything. Plus, we were armed to the teeth, with side-guns, pump-action Winchester rifles — all the genuine article. We went to a well known dude ranch outside Phoenix, where we took up with a guide called Sam Earp (a descendant of Wyatt), who took us to a place on the Apache reservation called Green River. The Apaches round there are all shepherds, and it was truly beautiful country. We set up a safe shooting range in a gully, and practiced with our Colt .45 revolvers. Those things are *impossible*! Not only does the kick nearly take your arm off, but you can't actually hit anything with them either. We stayed there overnight, cooking steaks and baked potatoes on an open fire, drinking beer, telling stories and singing songs... We were even woken by gunfire — a bobcat was trying to steal our food, and Sam Earp was shooting at it. Riding back to the ranch the next day we got caught in this fantastic flash flood, and Sam got us to help herd some cattle nearer to the ranch so they wouldn't get isolated — not only did I get to fulfill all my pop star fantasies on that tour — being chased by hordes of girls and so on — but I also got to live out every *Boys' Own* cowboy fantasy as well! The flight back to LA was hysterical. Apart from looking like the James gang, we stank to high heaven, having been in the saddle for 48 hours and nowhere near a bath. I assume we must have packed the guns away, otherwise I doubt if we'd have been let on the plane. Even so, we provoked some truly wonderful, horrified expressions, but once they knew 'we' were the Rolling Stones, it was OK.

"Back in LA, the band went into the studio for a week, to cut '19th Nervous Breakdown'. It was a very nice period for me — very relaxed, a lot of nice people around, like Lou Adler and Jack Nitzsche. We were staying at a great hotel, partying and going to clubs...a great way to wind down from the tour. The photos that I took in the studio ended up filling the booklet that came with the *High Tide & Green Grass* album.

"When I came back, my life had been changed. A lot of people within the music business knew that I'd been on the road with the Rolling Stones as their official photographer, so in a lot of people's minds I was now their official photographer, period. It didn't increase the offers of work noticeably, but it didn't exactly do my reputation any harm either. The whole thing was a great personal success.

"Over the next eighteen months or so, I photographed the Stones at home and in the studio whenever publicity shots were needed, and took another album cover photo, for *Between The Buttons*. I also saw a fair amount of them socially, 'though towards the end of my relationship with them we drifted apart quite a bit.

"The obvious question is: what were they like? And the answer is that they were nice people, they were my friends. Mick was charming and very funny, and a professional — he knew he wanted to be a star, and he worked very hard at it. He had fantastic charisma, and was very adept at managing publicity — he, Keith and Andrew would work out all these ways of manipulating the press, and Mick would carry them through. But the press loved it all — the Stones always provided good copy. He was definitely the Stones' spokesman. Mick and Keith were a fantastic team — they wrote well together, and they had a lot of fun together.

"If Mick was the public face of the Rolling Stones, then Keith was the soul of the band; in a way, Keith *was* the Rolling Stones. He was probably my closest mate within the band — always a lot of fun, really enthusiastic for whatever was going on. I suppose things were pretty innocent then — there was a high level of fun, and they were enjoying it all. They were breaking America, riding a crest — none of it was negative.

"Andrew was the other third of that team, definitely. He was the same age as them, as hip or hipper — he talked his own language, which was incomprehensible to outsiders...riddles and rhymes, and a million ideas at once. He was the one who got them writing together, who'd bounce ideas off them in the studio. And he loved being outrageous, attracting attention and then exploiting it...he was a master of 'image'.

"Bill and Charlie were...Bill and Charlie. Always there, always reliable. Bill used to get the mickey taken about his age, and the fact that he wasn't quite as fashionable as the others (who were *very* fashion conscious). I always got on well with him, but we didn't have a lot in common, even though he was quite keen on photography, even then.

SATISFACTION: THE ROLLING STONES BY GERED MANKOWITZ

He always looked as though he had something better to do, and like Charlie, he got on with the job — he was the 'moody stoneface', but in reality he wasn't moody at all. He just didn't smile very much. He has the reputation now of being the Stones' archivist, and he certainly has a phenomenal memory — he could place, date and name every lady he'd ever passed the night with, which was a considerable number. Bill was definitely a ladies' man. Charlie was a great friend, almost family. Very genuine, very funny, very quiet — he had a reputation for being a monosyllabic moron, which was a million miles from the truth. He just had no desire to get involved with the publicity machine, and was happiest at home with his wife. He wasn't interested in the glamour of rock at all, but he loved the comforts that the money brought him — he had terrific taste, in furniture, clothes, music...he took me to some great jazz clubs in New York. He was terribly keen to be a good drummer, and was always practicing complex finger exercises with his drumsticks — he didn't seem to rate himself very highly as a drummer, which is amazing, since he's considered one of the best there is. I really looked on him as an elder brother — he'd always tell you if you were a bit over the top: 'Past your bedtime, son'.

"The great thing about the Stones from my (professional) point of view was that they *were* the Stones — there was none of the smiling, eager to please image that the Beatles personified. The Stones didn't smile; they gave you fuck all to work with, other than what they *were* — which actually made them easy to photograph. Even Brian, who seemed to go out of his way to fuck pictures up, was just reinforcing his own image — the wicked gnome or the naughty boy, depending on how you looked at it. In a lot of photos he isolates himself from the rest of the group, apparently quite intentionally, and that was just an extension of his whole life. He certainly seemed to be the one most into 'other things', be they musical instruments, or ethnic cultures or new drugs. He had his own circle of friends, and lived an almost twilight life. He was definitely the least normal. He was superficially very easy to get on with, very polite...but almost impossible to get through to. There was a manipulative, slightly unpleasant quality about him, and if anybody was going to fuck things up generally, it would be Brian — apparently he'd always been that way. He'd be late, he'd disappear — the band would actually play gigs without him: 'Sorry, Brian's got 'flu'. Sometimes he'd play terribly, to the point that Stew would just get furious with him and start shaking him physically, telling him to pull himself together. He could drive everybody potty, but when he was on form, he was a part of the team, and no matter what condition he was in, he was a brilliant musician — he could play anything. But by the time of the *Satanic Majesties* sessions, he was a pathetic mess — really stoned and really ill. He'd fall over, fall asleep in his food...and nobody could really do anything for him...even if they could have done, he'd alienated so many people by then, that I suppose it was too late. But he could still play — they sometimes had to prop him up on cushions, but he could still play brilliantly. A great musician, but a wreck of a human being — it's sad to even think about it.

"Of course, the weight was coming down on Brian, and on Mick and Keith, through the drugs busts. I remember joints being passed around at Olympic during the *Satanic Majesties* sessions, rolled in HM Prison issue rolling papers, but the joke was a bit thin. It was very serious; Andrew's office was in chaos, and it seemed like all the media was against them. There was a sense of general public outrage — 'get the Stones' — and I think we all thought they were going down for a long time. Les Perrin, the publicist, did a fantastic job of restraining the press from being even worse than they were and everybody near the Stones was told to be low-key, to keep out of the way, so as not to give the press any more ammunition.

"There was a great sense of relief when they were let out of jail. But towards the end, I found myself becoming alienated from Mick and Keith as people quite rapidly. They were getting involved with a lot of new fads, new people, and they were completely stoned most of the time — they'd changed enormously within the space of two years. They weren't my only rock clients — certainly they were the most important ones, but there were other things demanding my attention, and I wasn't prepared to become a part of the sycophantic entourage that was building up around them. I wasn't prepared to get involved with drugs to the extent that they seemed to be getting involved — it just seemed to be completely insane; I'd seen what their whole lifestyle had done to Brian, and Mick and Keith seemed intent on catching up with him. It didn't appeal to me. And the other aspects of their social scene, I couldn't keep up with — I didn't want to go to certain clubs and restaurants, simply because I couldn't afford to pick up my own tab.

"And it seemed that they were trying to force Andrew out. I'd become increasingly friendly with Andrew — when he was in good form, he was great fun, and a terrific person to work for — he got me to do some of the best, most inspired work I'd ever done. He had great ideas, but could still give you almost complete freedom to interpret them. When he was off, he was way off, and it was best to stay away, but otherwise he was a lot of fun. As things with the Stones got worse, I was definitely closer to Andrew than to them, and it turned out that there were definitely two camps. At the *Satanic Majesties* sessions, the band would turn up later and later each night, and achieve less and less — they'd arrive either really morose, or totally stoned. I think even Bill and Charlie were pissed off with it — Andrew was *really* pissed off, because he couldn't get anything done, and they were running thousands of pounds over budget; he turned round several times and said 'This is ridiculous. What am I doing here?' It was all quite unpleasant...time-consuming, exhausting, tense, unproductive. I was there because Andrew wanted me to photograph the sessions, and you could feel all these undercurrents going on. The end, when it came was really quite traumatic. A recent member of the Stones' entourage was a photographer called Michael Cooper, and at one of the recording sessions he approached Andrew and said 'Mick's asked me to talk to you about the new album cover'. I knew instantly that I was out, and I think it was the final straw for Andrew as well — that the cover should have been seriously discussed without his opinion was a sign that he was no longer part of things; from then on, it was just a question of negotiation.

"For my part, that was pretty much it — I didn't bother going to the studio again. I still saw Mick and Keith once in a while, as I was still friends with Marianne. I saw Charlie once in a while socially. I even photographed Mick a couple of times for various magazines. But basically my relationship with them had ended by the winter of 1967. After then, whatever they did, I was obviously aware of it, and viewed it in the light of the time I'd known them. I preferred to remember them as they were on that American tour — young and enjoying it, and still a part of the real world." *Gered Mankowitz, London, 1984.*

ON STAGE AMERICA, 1965

"I really love the picture on the right. It had never been printed till recently, and it was a real find. I always wanted to show the relationship between the band and the audience — the audiences fascinated me. It was difficult because I was totally dependent on whatever lighting there was at the gig, and that varied enormously."

"These (below) really capture something of the energy and the hysteria of the audiences. Onstage with the band, you can't help but feel the centre of attention, and to look out at reactions like these is a very strange feeling. You can see the sheer presence of police, security and first aid people here — the authorities didn't know how to handle it at all."

ON STAGE AMERICA, 1965

ON STAGE AMERICA, 1965

Opposite: "An amazing bit of Jagger. The thing lying at his feet is not a dead fan, but a huge doll that came hurtling up with a message pinned to it. It was more usually bras or panties, with invitations to parties, or offers of an extremely rude nature."

ON STAGE AMERICA, 1965

ON STAGE AMERICA, 1965

"Two gigs that got stopped (below). In the first photo, you can see the sherriff stopping the concert; in the second, Mick is already stirring the audience up again — sometimes concerts would be stopped three or four times before the authorities lost patience and stopped the thing altogether. In the third photo, once again the concert had been stopped — the character on the far right is Pete Bennett, the record plugger. The problem with the audience rushing the stage was that the band sometimes got hurt — they'd be scratched or bruised, and have their clothes torn — it happened unintentionally, but it happened quite often. More often, the kids themselves got hurt."

ON STAGE AMERICA, 1965

"This was another concert that actually got stopped. The reason for the strange lighting is that the whole concert was lit by one huge light. The audience had begun to break through the cordon, and you can sense how close they are to the stage; then they actually broke through, and the police were backed up against the stage. The sherriff came on stage, and ordered the audience to cool it; then the plug was — literally — pulled, and the concert stopped...that's why the band are all looking into the wings. The safety curtain was brought down (that's the wrinkled background), and Brian and Keith proceeded to have a go at the sherriff. In the final shot, the person waving his hands in the air in the pale jacket is Andrew; on his left, also in a pale jacket, is Jerry Brandt from the William Morris Agency, and on the far left is Pete Bennett, the record plugger. They were all trying to reason with the sherriff, but it didn't work. The concert was over.

ON STAGE AMERICA, 1965

Fans rush stage, Washington DC, 13th November 1965:
"This is all happending really quickly, and the level of hysteria is difficult to communicate. One minute the band is playing, then three or four girls jumped onstage and began molesting Brian — you can see that Bill and Keith are still harmonising, but Mick's distracted. The character in the pale jacket trying to hustle the girls away is Bob Bowness. The motorcycle cop in the foreground is about to pull a gun on me and order me off stage ('and knock off the Limey accent'). Fortunately, Andrew was behind me in the wings, and he somehow convinced him that I really was with the band."

ON STAGE AMERICA, 1965

Above, handicapped fans in wheelchairs, before the concert: "Anybody in a wheelchair was automatically placed at the front of the audience. It was obviously great that they were able to come, but it was a bit embarrassing for us — they'd be the first sight you'd see when you came onstage, and they were inevitably the subject of some pretty sick jokes at the time."

Left: "Bill told me that the reason he'd adopted this moody way of playing bass — holding the neck straight up — was so that he could shade his eyes from the spotlights with the neck, and be able to see all the girls in the front row. You could see him pulling the girls while he was still on stage, mouthing his room number at them."

Opposite, Vancouver: "This was an ice hockey stadium, with a really high stage for the band. I selected the picture for several reasons...Brian played harmonica, which was always kind of a highspot...that's not the audience behind the stage, but press photographers, and they're obviously as fascinated by the behaviour of the fans as I was...and finally, it really shows off the police presence — that row of helmets below the stage looks really sinister."

ON STAGE AMERICA, 1965

Top: "Brian's image was pretty and cute — 'sweet li'l innocent Brian', the fans used to call out. I think it was a nickname dreamt up by 16 magazine. It's hard to imagine anybody less innocent."

Above: Charlie's introduction. "This was a regular part of the act. Mick would say 'And now I'd like to introduce you to our drummer', and Charlie would step up to the mike and say, for instance, ''ullo New York, I'm Charlie'."

ON STAGE AMERICA, 1965

ON STAGE AMERICA, 1965

Left: "Charlie was always difficult to photograph onstage, partly because he was virtually unlit, and partly because he was concentrating so hard that he normally had his eyes shut, with his head down. You can see here that whenever a gig was at a theatre, there was always a crowd of people in the wings."

Opposite, Andrew Loog Oldham backstage: "Last minute chaos, the band tuning up. The guy on the far right in the pale jacket was Bob Bowness, the tour manager."

ON STAGE AMERICA, 1965

ON STAGE AMERICA, 1965

Above: "Mick used the tambourine and maraccas to tease the audience...he'd really use them to get the girls going like mad."

Left: "Mick and Brian both have great expressions on their faces here. The bored guys leaning on the stage are Ivy League students, roped in for the night as local security."

ON STAGE AMERICA, 1965

Fort Worth, Texas: "This is one unedited roll of film. The venue was a huge auditorium that was used for various sports, and the stage was right in the middle of the arena, so in order to get from the dressing room to the stage, they were put in an armoured car and driven there. After I took the first picture of Brian and Bill eating hot dogs in the dressing room, I ran out front and got into position by the stage, so as to record their arrival. From frame 3 onwards you can see the truck slowly moving up, and the audience getting more and more excited — like the girl with the camera, who's running back and forth. The moment the van appeared, the screaming started... absolutely deafening. You can get a sense of the frantic rush as the door opens, with the police linking arms and making a line to hold the fans back. That's Bob Bowness getting out first in frame 14, followed by Brian, then Keith (16) and Mick (17) and finally Charlie...I must have missed Bill — all this happened really fast. Next they're on stage, and in frame 20 is Ian 'Stew' Stewart, piano player and master roadie...the '6th Stone'."

ON STAGE AMERICA, 1965

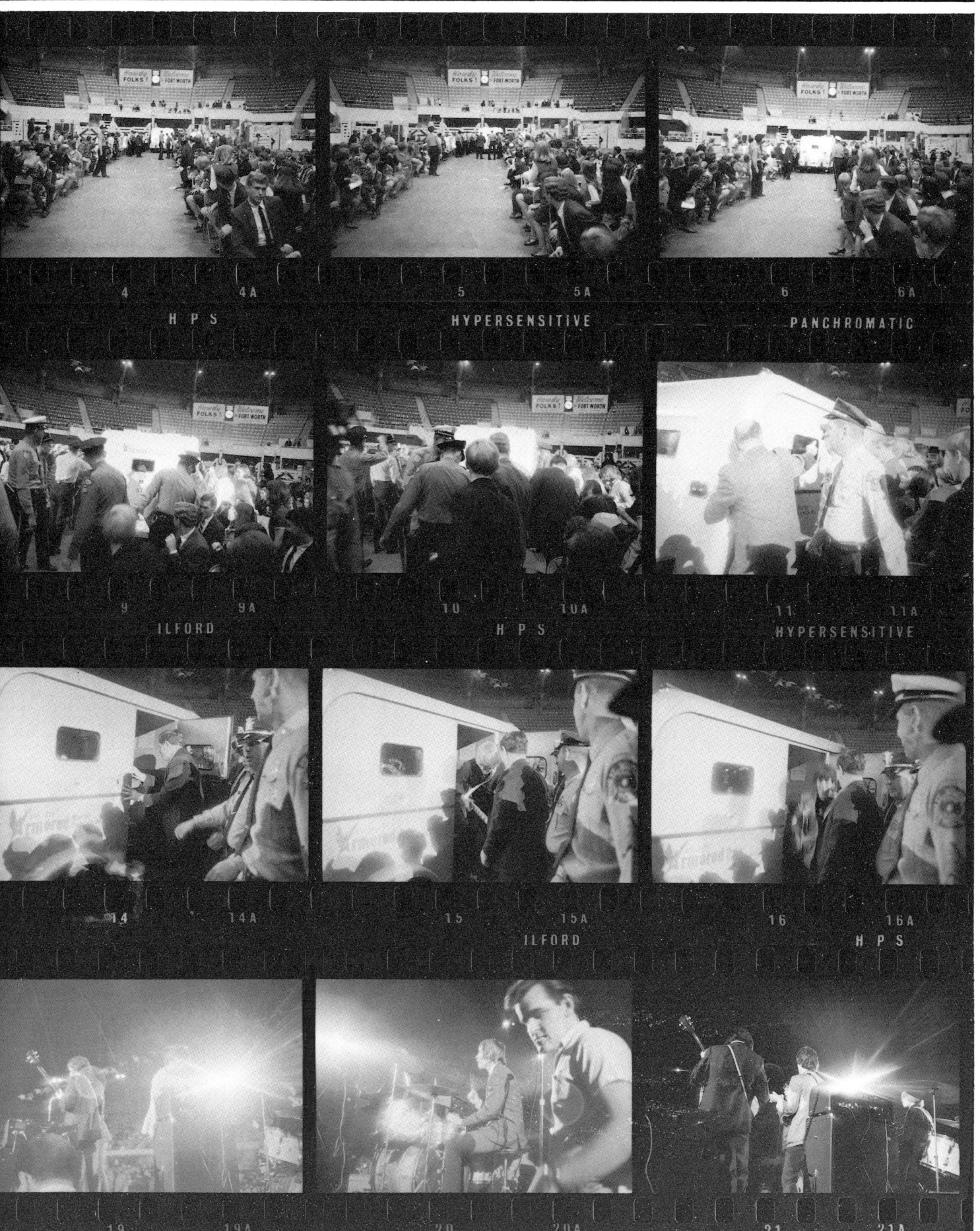

ON STAGE AMERICA, 1965

"It was virtually impossible to get good live group shots, so I concentrated on doing lots of individual portraits. I chose not to use flash, and tried to capture as much of the natural excitement as possible."

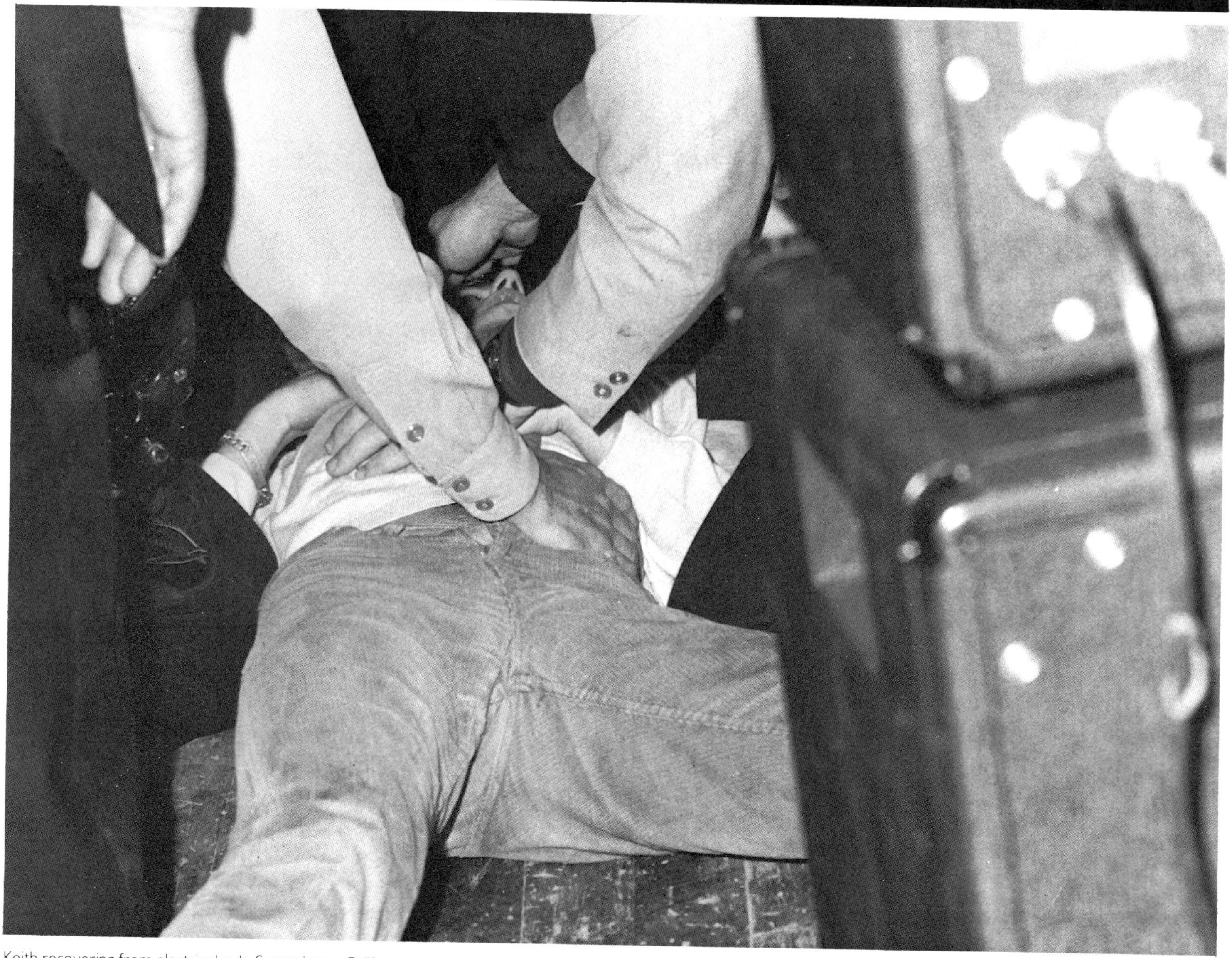

BACK STAGE AMERICA, 1965

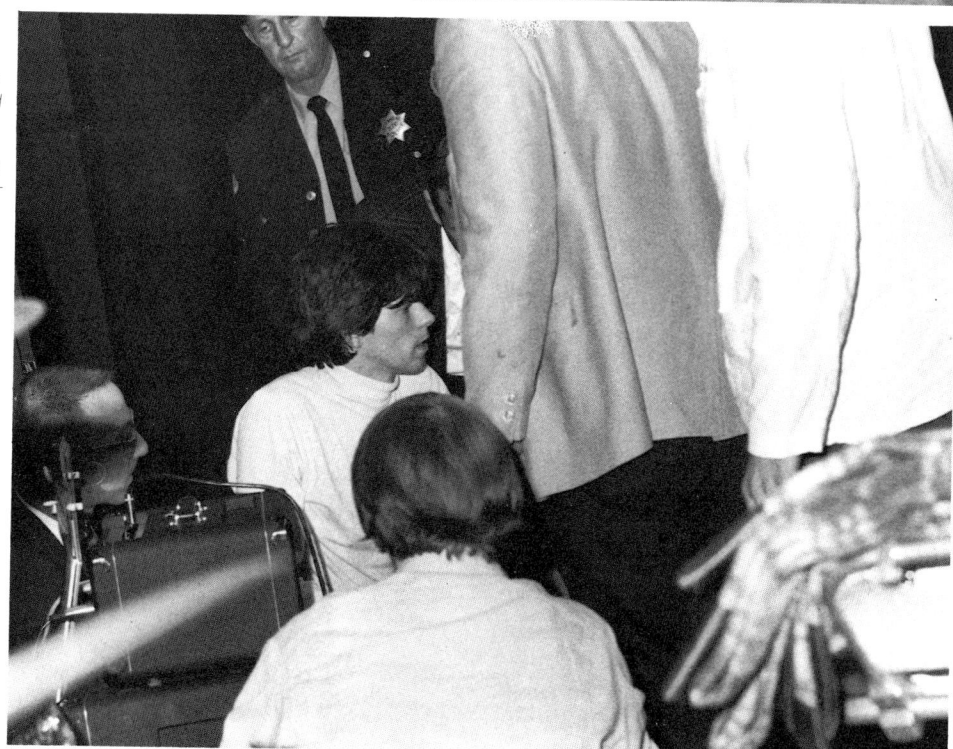

Keith recovering from electric shock, Sacramento, California, 4th December 1965: *"His microphone had slipped around, so that it wasn't facing him, and he tried to push it back into place with the neck of his guitar. The thing couldn't have been properly earthed, because the metal guitar strings touching the mike stand completed a circuit — there was a flash and a bang, and Keith was flung the entire depth of the stage, right up to the back line amps. The curtain came down immediately, and there was chaos everywhere. I think everybody on stage thought Keith was dead — he was motionless and absolutely white. I wasn't taking pictures, because Keith was my friend...it was my friend lying there. There were a lot of people around him...Bob Bowness, security men, police, band members — the theatre manager, shitting himself in case he got sued — I was just trying to see what was going on. When it was clear that Keith was alive, somebody said 'Why aren't you taking pictures? Take some pictures.' I must somehow have had a flashgun on me, and I took these two...one of Keith lying flat out (above), and one a minute or so later (right), as he was sitting up and recovering. He got up and seemed to recover very quickly — even joked about it. The sense of relief onstage was overwhelming — we'd genuinely thought he'd died. Apparently he was out for seven minutes, and they went on to finish the concert — I don't remember. I was too shaken up."*

BACK STAGE AMERICA, 1965

Bo Diddley, Chicago: "Bo Diddley was added to the bill for a couple of gigs, as an added attraction. Here (above), he's concentrating on his toffee apple, while the band sift through the presents and notes that have piled up backstage. Bo's sister, the Duchess, had a small monkey that rode around on her shoulder and kept trying to bite people — it certainly made you keep your distance from her. The Stones always got on well with black musicians — they were regarded as 'soul brothers'. Even in Harlem, when we went to see James Brown live, or down South, when we went to see Solomon Burke in a tiny club, and we were literally the only white people there, it was cool. People understood that the Stones cared about the music."

Left, card game with Patti Labelle & The Bluebells: "That's Nona Hendryx on the right, and Patti's hand in the foreground. This really sums up for me the atmosphere on the tour — very happy."

BACK STAGE AMERICA, 1965

"A typical dressing room — a real shithole. There was always a lot of fan presence backstage...friends of the promoter, prizewinners from radio contests, kids who'd bribed the security men... they always got in somehow. It was quite a struggle sometimes to be polite to them, but the band were usually very nice. When it was obviously getting a bit too much, somebody would break it up — 'sorry, but the boys have got to get ready now'. You can see a girl holding the tour programme for this tour, with my 'cage' shot on the cover."

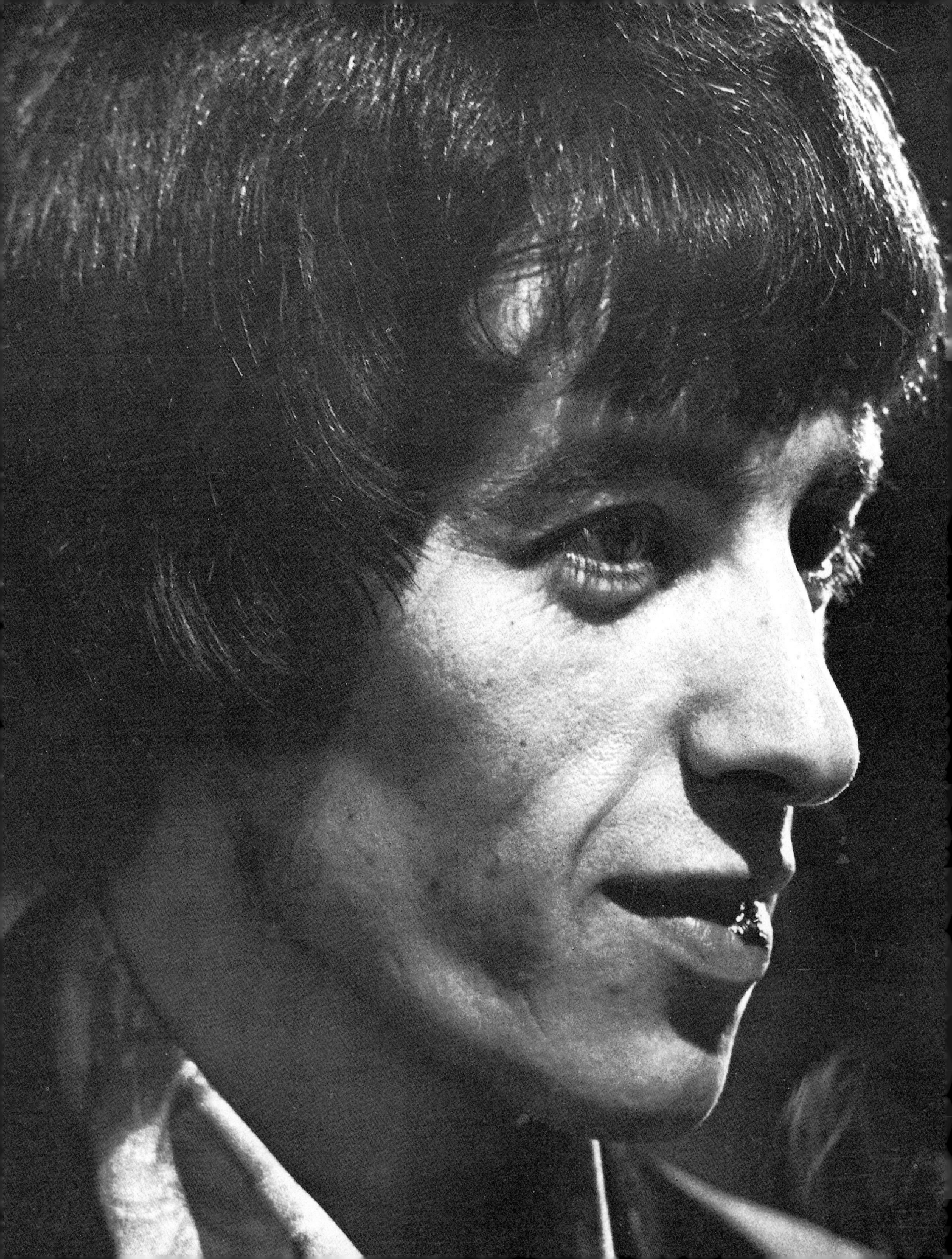

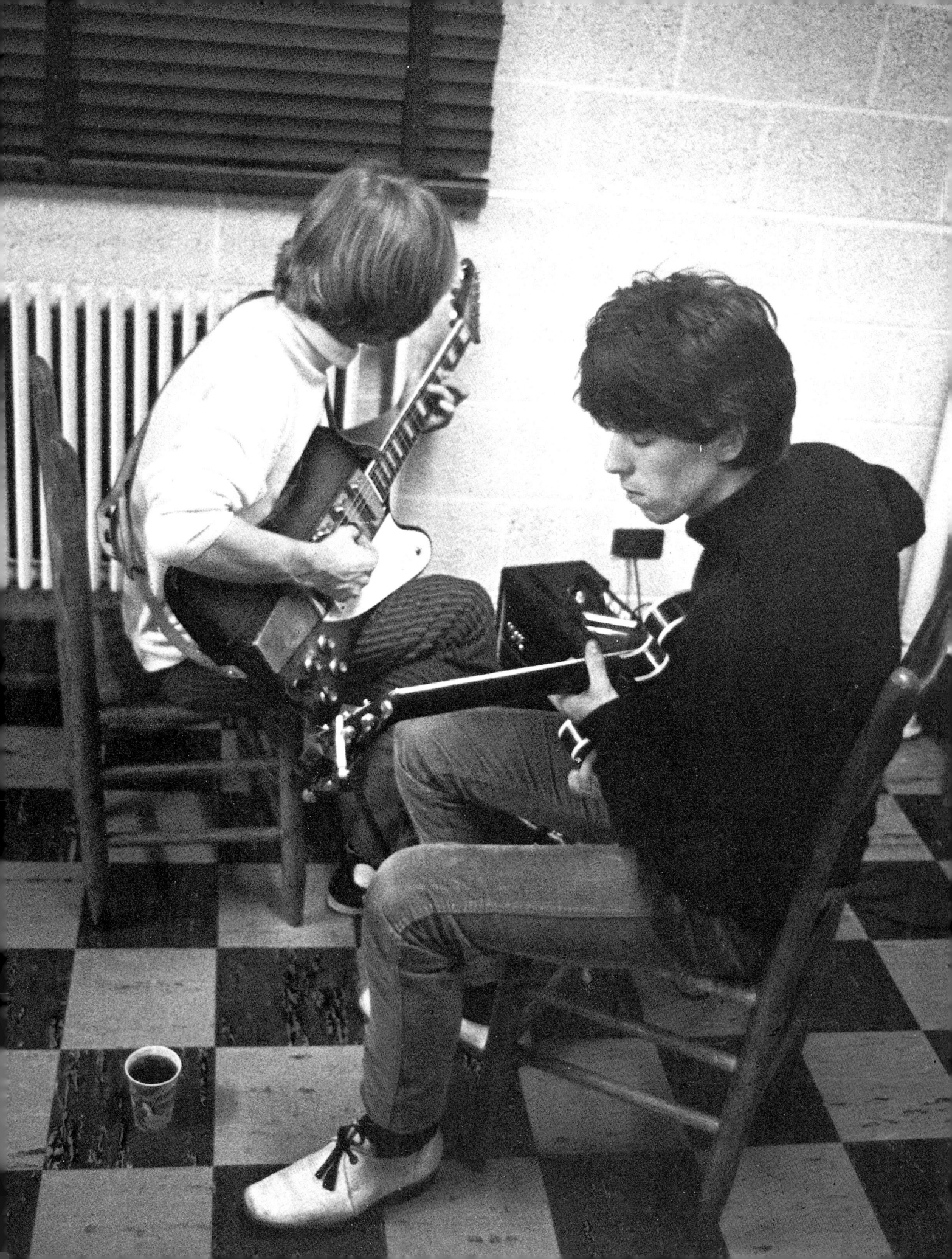

BACK STAGE AMERICA, 1965

"The lull before the storm...spending hours in a dressing room that was pretty short on comfort, just waiting for something to happen. Often local TV and radio stations would actually create awards, as a way of getting an interview with the Stones. If they rang up the theatre manager and said 'The Rolling Stones have just been voted the best 5-piece long-haired English group of the week by our viewers/listeners, and we'd like to present them with an award', the theatre would go along with it, because it was good publicity. The awards nearly always looked like bowling trophies."

BACK STAGE AMERICA, 1965

"The police who were to look after the dressing room often relaxed and joined us for a drink. They'd show us their guns, start telling stories...by the end of a couple of hours they'd be quite friendly... they'd turn a blind eye to the odd joint, ask for autographs for their kids.... In the States you can actually hire the services of the police, at an hourly rate, and it wasn't unusual for us to hire a police escort to and from the airport. In one town, the police stopped us leaving the concert because they'd been told to keep the road clear for the band — not realising we were the band. Once down South, a motorcycle outrider drew level with us on his huge police Harley-Davidson, doing about 60 mph, with his feet on the handlebars and combing his hair — real Southern maccho. The whole relationship with the cops was quite curious, but there were never any major conflicts."

Top: "Bill, Mick, Bob Bowness (tour manager) and Andrew. To avoid security problems, we always got to gigs hours early, so there was always time to kill. Nothing much to do but chat and eat."

Above: "It seemed like every town had a small local TV station, and several radio stations, that wanted to do interviews — this is a typical scene...they almost always happened in the dressing room before the gig. The media in America is really localized, and the Stones coming to town was always big news. The band's reactions to all this were pretty good. Mick was always the one they wanted to talk to, and he definitely was the spokesman — and he gave them good copy."

BACK STAGE AMERICA, 1965

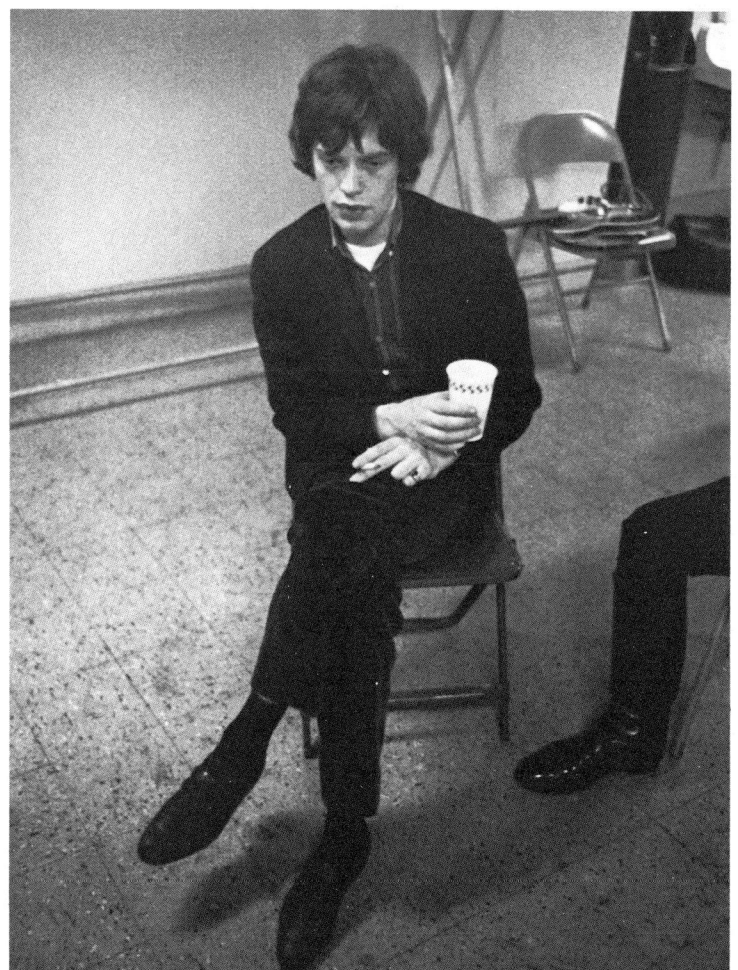

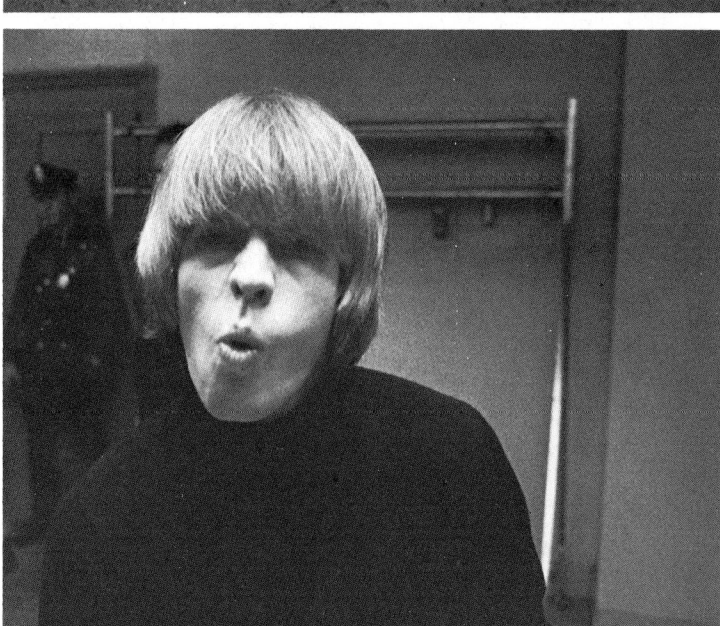

Above, Brian pulls 'semi-nanker': "A 'nanker' was a horrific face you'd pull to frighten children, policemen and so on. It involved using both hands to pull back your eyelids, nostrils and mouth. This is a somewhat half-hearted version — 'no hands'."

"God knows what these sinks were designed for, but it wasn't people. I think Charlie had the right idea."

TIME OFF IN AMERICA, 1965

Above, Colorado, December 1965: "We went riding several times, and this was the first. We had a bit of spare time, and Keith and Charlie had decided to go riding. Charlie, knowing I liked riding, invited me along. Beautiful countryside — that's my horse on the left. 'Do Not Run Horses' means don't gallop."

Left, Keith and Ronnie Schneider, Arizona, December 1965: "Keith's Billy the Kid image. The black horse was Ronnie's. When we got to the campsite, we let the horses stop for a drink in the nearby stream. Ronnie's horse decided to have a roll in the water — with Ronnie still on it!"

DEPARTURE FROM LONDON, 1965

VIP Lounge, Heathrow Airport, 27 October 1965
"Waiting for the plane. Bill's wife and Anita Pallenberg had come to say goodbye; Mick read about the Beatles' MBEs; Charlie looked slightly down, probably because of leaving Shirley."

MID-ATLANTIC, 1965

46

MID-ATLANTIC, 1965

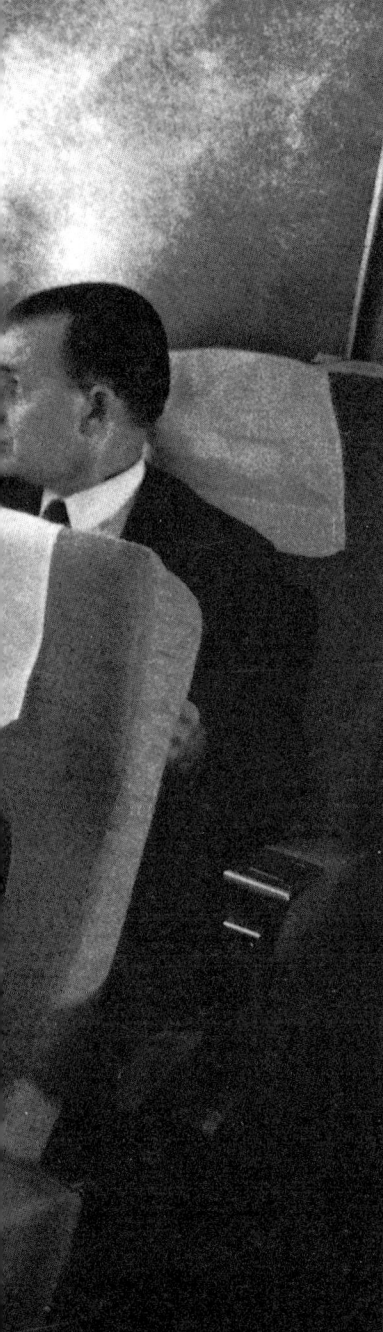

TWA First Class, Royal Ambassador Service, London to New York, 27 October 1965 "Killing time for eight hours: (opposite left) Mick and Keith check the programme for the inflight movie; (top right) Brian displays the first of many American beers; (top far right) Charlie gets involved with the Saturday Evening Post; (right) Stew gets his head down into a book.

MID-ATLANTIC, 1965

"The young man with the glasses is me, as photographed by Mick Jagger."

"This sequence starts off with a card game on the plane, then cuts to our arrival in New York — I got off first, to be able to take these shots. I'd seen all the classic shots of bands waving as they came down the steps, and wanted to try something along those lines. Fortunately, Brian started messing about with his bags, which is a nice touch. The Stones weren't cut out for wearing matching suits and waving anyway. The person at the bottom of the steps is a very bewildered TWA official, and the person in the cardigan behind the band is Stew — the people at the top of the steps are just rather annoyed first class passengers, who are being delayed by this unruly pop group. The last photos were taken in the limo, en route to Manhattan."

MID-ATLANTIC, 1965

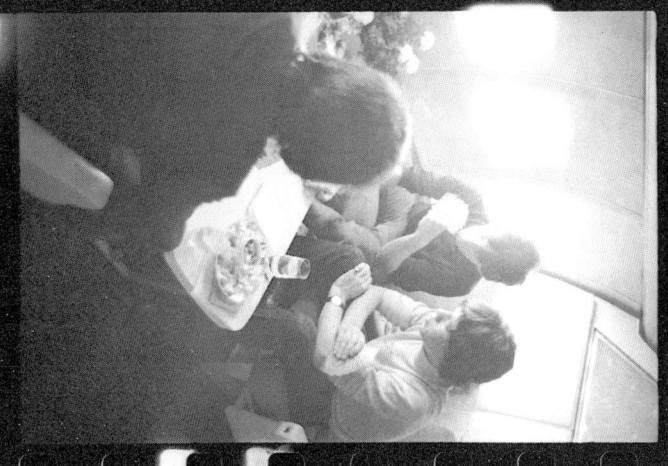

N.B.C. TELEVISION NEW YORK, 1965

Taping 'Hullabaloo' TV show New York, November 1965: *"I wasn't allowed on to the studio floor for the actual taping. This was the only national TV spot they did that tour."*

Opposite: *"Brian had his hair cut first, by the studio barber."*

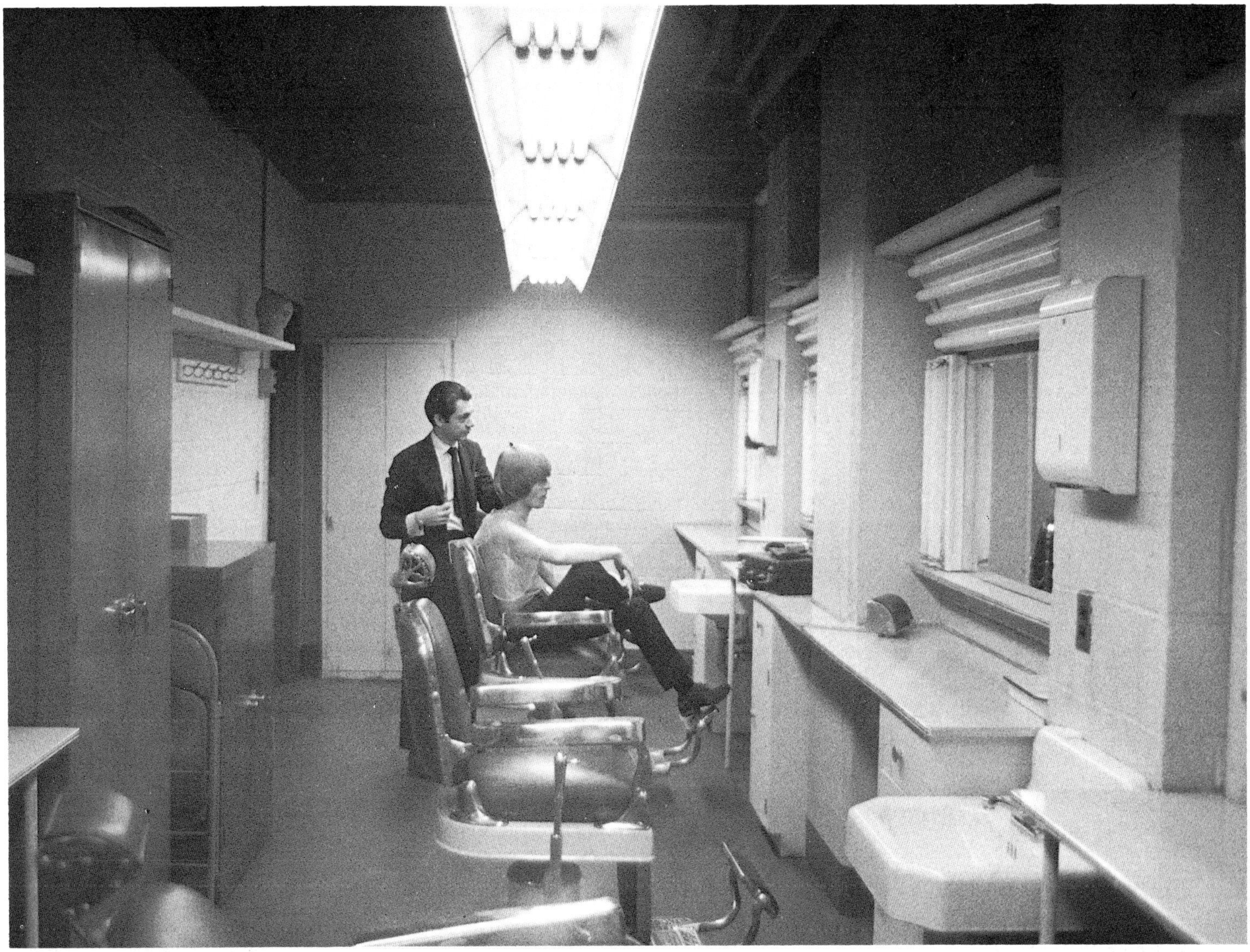

N.B.C. TELEVISION NEW YORK, 1965

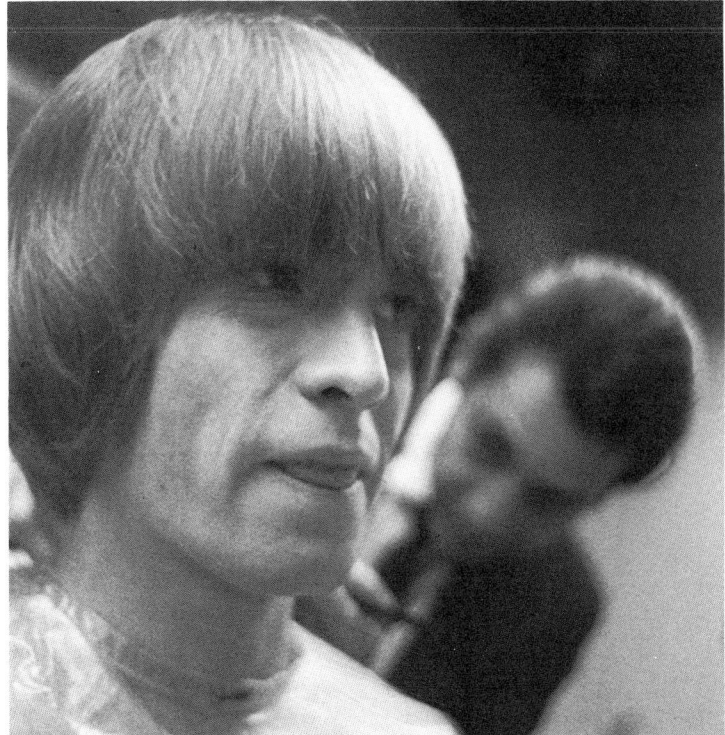

THE FIRST SESSION: LONDON, APRIL 1965

Masons Yard, London April 1965 *"My first session with the Stones, taken on a building site adjacent to my studio in Masons Yard, Piccadilly. There was very definitely a 'Stones fashion', of which Brian and Mick were obvious examples — Keith's the only one here wearing jeans. Brian really favoured white trousers, with roll neck sweaters. Or else check trousers — the 'Rupert the Bear' image. I know people today who would pay a fortune for Brian's shoes."*

THE FIRST SESSION: LONDON, APRIL 1965

THE FIRST SESSION: LONDON, APRIL 1965

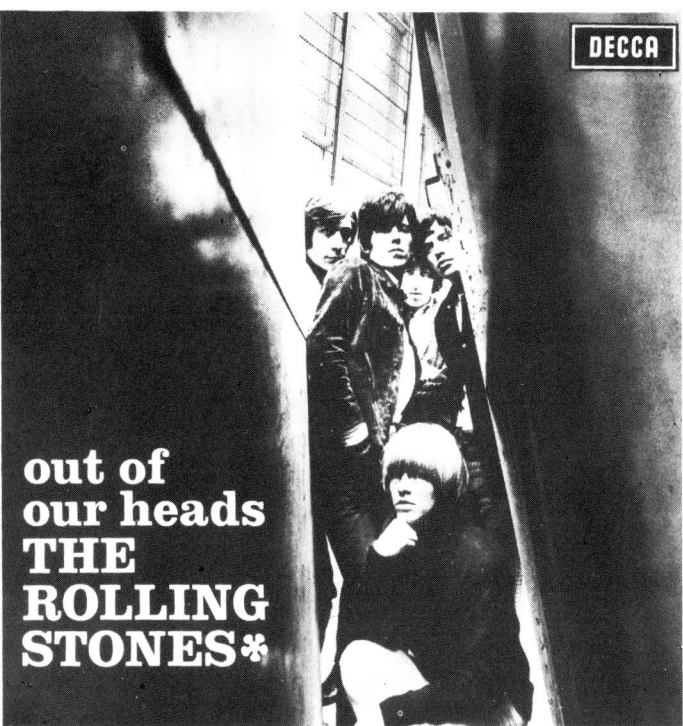

Top, Masons Yard, London, April 1965: "One of my favourite Stones pictures of all time, and used on the cover of the Autumn '65 tour programme. The cage was a bit of 'found poetry' — it was actually used for moving bricks around the building site. I used it to 'cage' the wild men of rock."

Above, Out Of Our Heads/December's Children: "It was wonderful for me to have a photo like this used as a cover. It broke a lot of rules, by not giving equal space to the band members. It was very unusual for the time, the people loved it."

LONDON, APRIL 1965

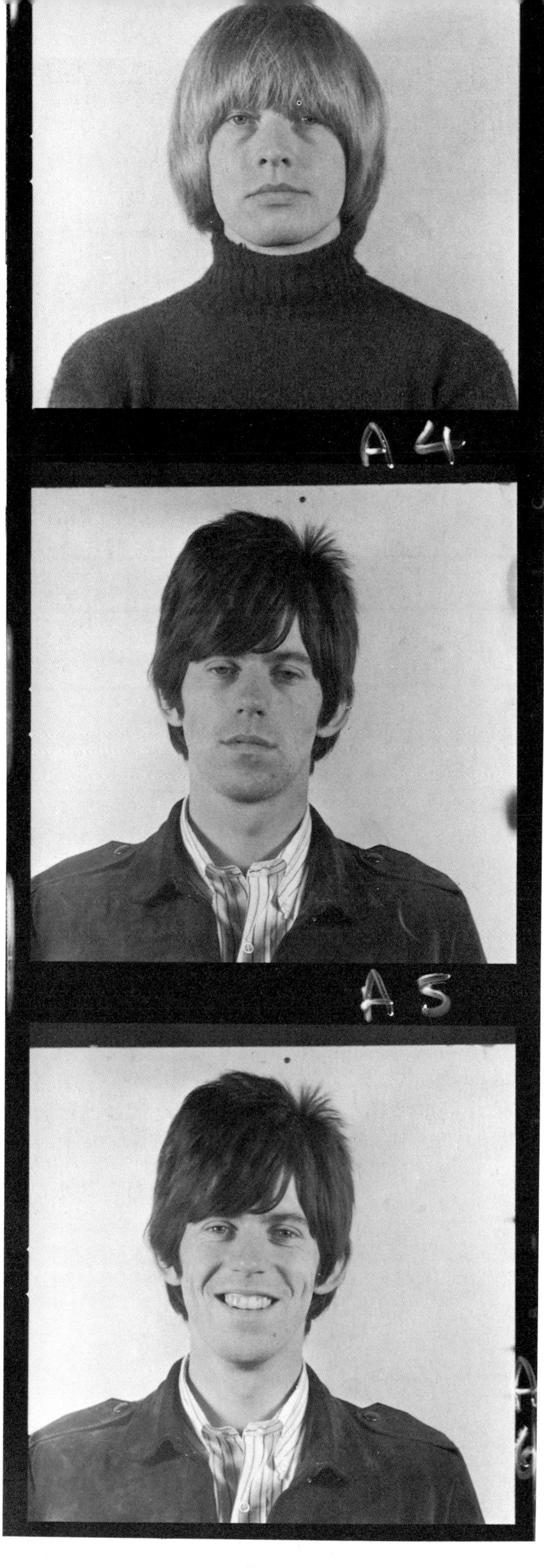

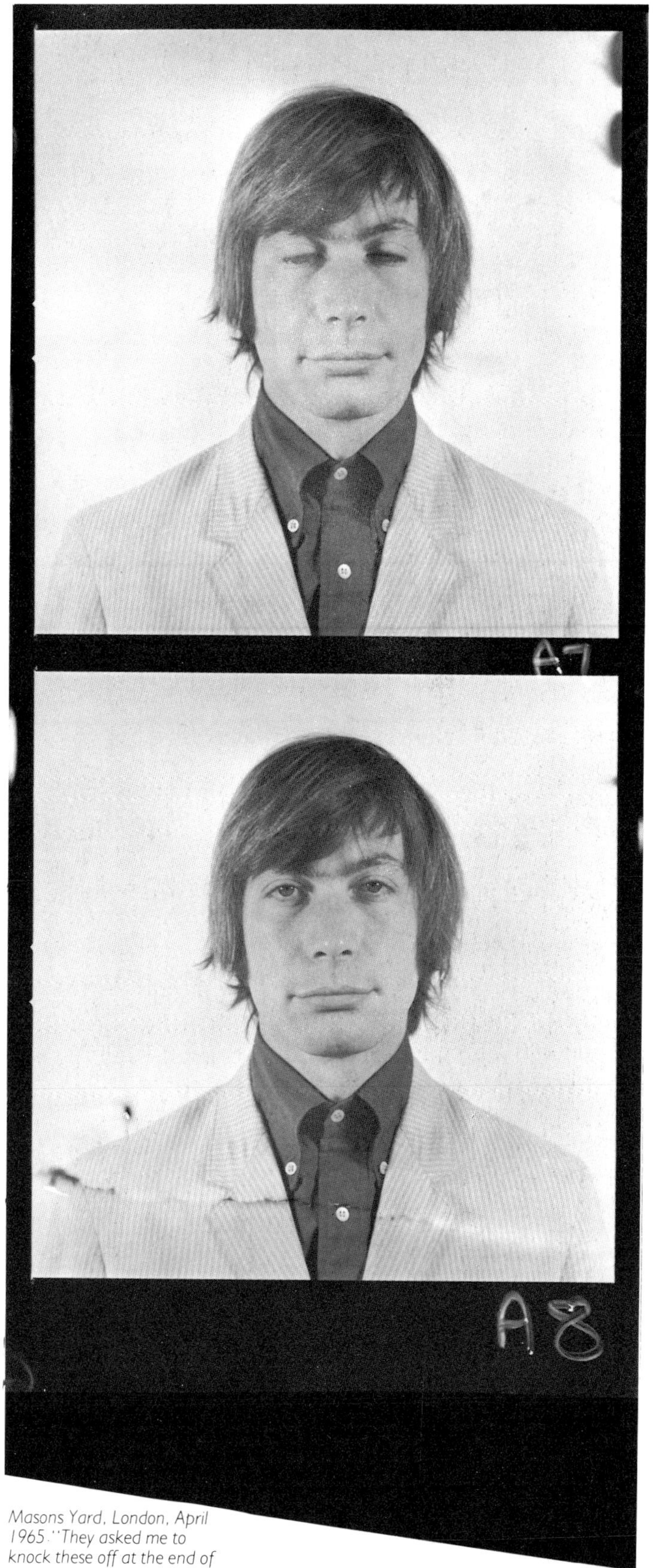

Masons Yard, London, April 1965. "They asked me to knock these off at the end of the first studio session I ever did with them — they needed them for their U.S. visa applications...I guess Bill already had his. It really phased me doing these really flat, boring portraits — not my scene at all. They're pretty awful, but quite interesting."

THE FIRST SESSION: LONDON, APRIL 1965

Masons Yard, April 1965: "Taken in my studio just before the outdoor shots, and the very first photos I did of the Stones."

AT HOME, ENGLAND 1966

"There was a lot of pressure on Andrew to supply the press with pictures of the band at home, so rather than have dozens of photographers invading their privacy, we organised these sessions. The reason that there are no shots of Brian is simply because his domestic life was pretty unstable at the time — he was living in several different places, and didn't have a 'home' as such, in the way that the others did."

"The star trip was definitely not for Charlie; he couldn't help taking the piss out of it. Both Charlie and Shirley painted in the little studio they had in the loft of the house — he couldn't take the photo session seriously at all. Note Shirley hanging out of the window."

AT HOME, ENGLAND 1966

"Photographing Bill at home was quite difficult, because the place was very formal, and Bill himself is so low-key. We were a bit desperate for subject matter, as you can see. He really came alive playing the keyboards; I think he liked the idea of being photographed playing them — it made a change from always being seen with a bass."

AT HOME, ENGLAND 1966

"Keith's house Redlands was set in beautiful Sussex countryside, which he absolutely loved. He'd just moved into the place, and it was being done up — the new plumbing hadn't been connected yet, so we did this 'Lord of the Manor' shot with the new loo. Quite a famous photo.

There was a large stream in the garden, that emptied into a small lake. I suggested that we take some shots of Keith rowing in this small dinghy. He kept going round in circles — note the ever-present fag in mouth.

It took Keith a long time to get the place the way he wanted it. In the meantime, he lived in two rooms, and was really happy 'camping' in his manor house. He really looks the archetypal bohemian."

AT HOME, ENGLAND 1966

"A hallway in Harley House, a very smart apartment building in Marylebone Road. Mick had just bought a place here, and although he was still living in his mews flat, he wanted to be photographed here, because this was going to be his home. He really looks at home in the Regency surroundings. You can see all the elements of an elegant flat taking shape — the beautiful mirror and the studded leather sofa."

MOBILE STONES, ENGLAND, 1966

"The inevitable—for the time—'pop star with car' photos. (Top left) Bill with his MGB, outside his house in South London. (Top right) Mick with Aston Martin outside his mews flat, near Gloucester Place. (Right) Keith outside Redlands, with Bentley Continental. The car went virtually everywhere with him. (Above) Charlie didn't drive, but Shirley Watts rode, so this seemed an appropriate substitute. Taken in the garden of their house in Lewes, Sussex.

ON STAGE, LONDON, 1966

Rehearsal for TV appearance on 'Sunday Night At The London Palladium', 22 January 1967: "I wasn't allowed to take pictures during the actual show, I think because I was with the Stones, rather than a press photographer. They performed the B-side of their new single, 'Ruby Tuesday' (you can see the double bass, that Bill used, on the left), but I think the A-side, 'Let's Spend The Night Together' was banned because it was too suggestive. You can clearly see the revolving stage here — at the end of each show it was a tradition for all the performers to stand on the revolving stage and wave goodnight to the audience. The Stones refused to do this, and it caused a real outrage at the time — it was an insult to showbusiness. It was great."

BACK STAGE, LONDON, 1966

Above, signing autograph books brought from stage door, London Palladium: "You can tell this was done 'live' on a Sunday by the vicar on TV — this was 'the Godslot'."

Left, dressing room, London Palladium: "Les Perrin, the Stones' legendary publicist, can be glimpsed in the mirror."

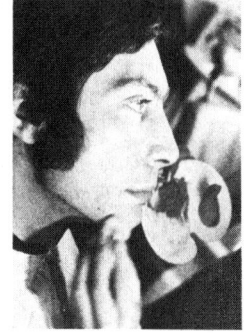

"Charlie has some attention from the make-up girl."

BACK STAGE, LONDON, 1966

Before the show, London Palladium dressing room, 22 January 1967: "I usually avoided photographing the Stones with joints, partly because the pictures wouldn't be publishable, and partly because it would have undermined their confidence in me if they'd seen me taking those sort of pictures. But by this time, it was no big deal for Mick to make jokes about snorting from bottles, or for Keith to be seen smoking a joint and a cigarette...these were still private photos anyway. I think they were pretty wired up — they already knew they weren't going to go on the revolving stage. That was all planned from the start — it was either Andrew's idea or Mick's. They were going to make it an event...'the Rolling Stones' Sunday Night At The London Palladium'."

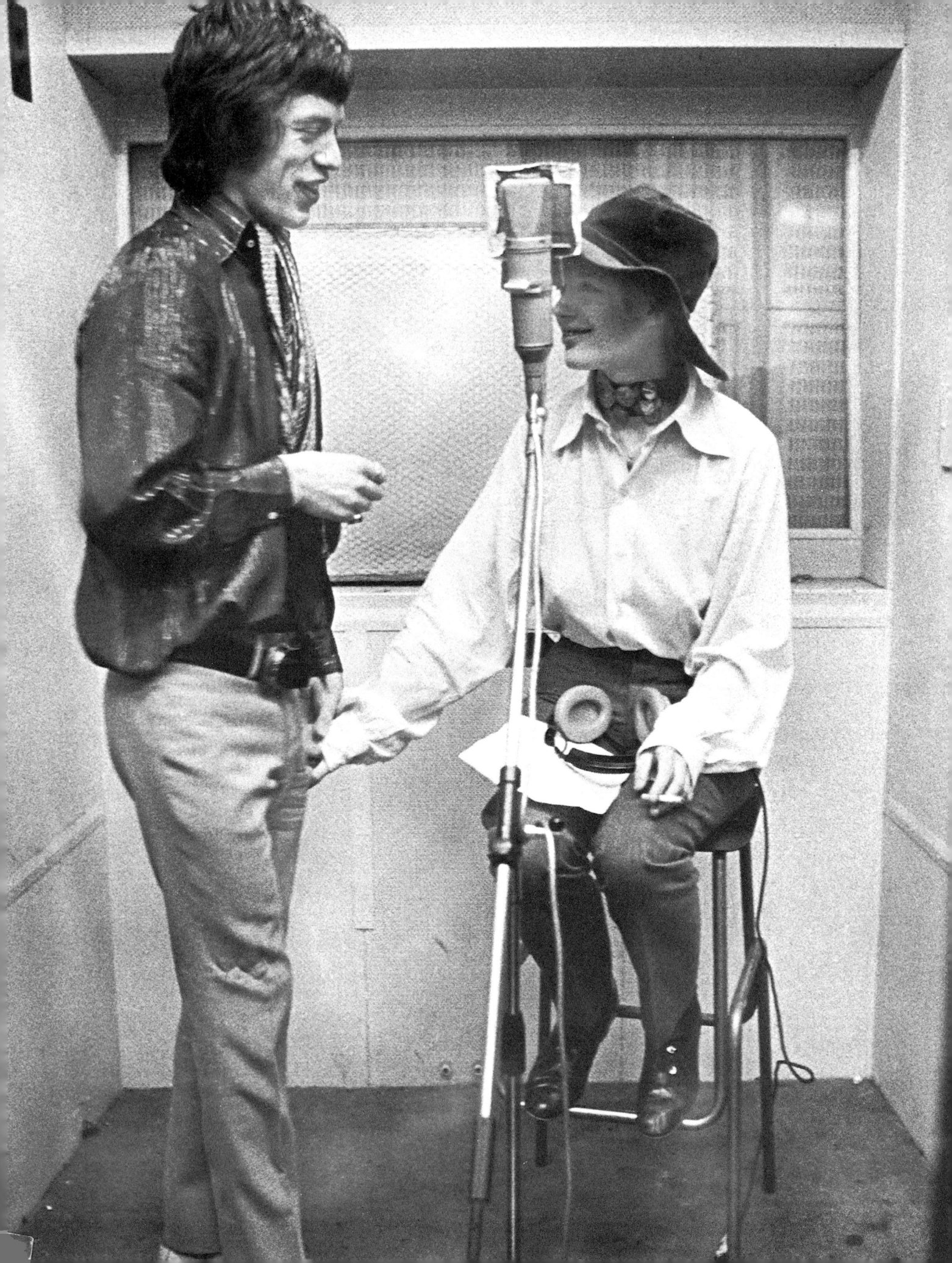

MICK RECORDS MARIANNE, LONDON, 1967

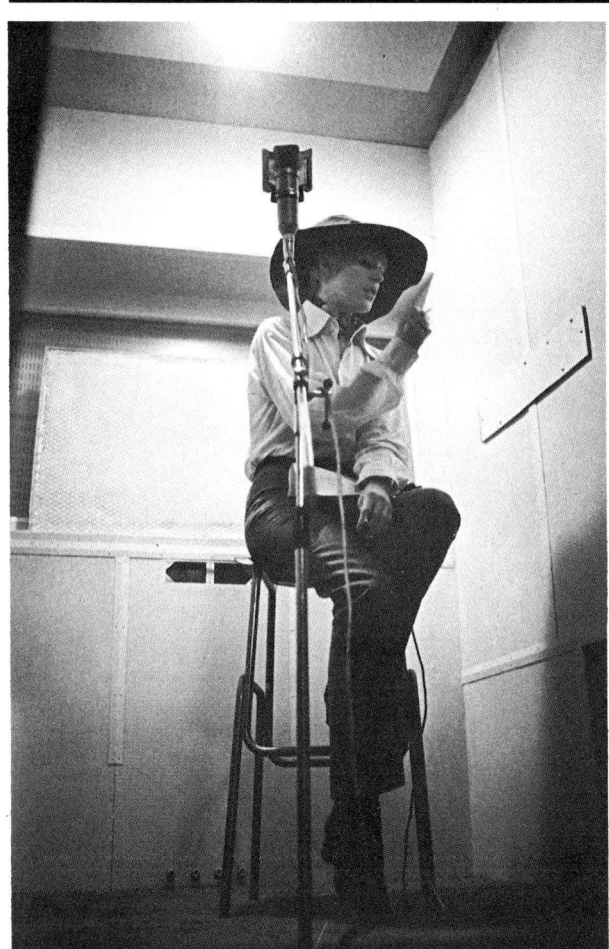

Marianne Faithfull recording session, Decca Studios, London, February 1967
"Mick was really sweet with Marianne in those days. In Bristol, on the English tour in October '66, I remember Marianne coming up to me and saying how great Mick was looking. Half an hour later, Mick came up to me to tell me how great Marianne was looking. Hours later, I saw them outside, holding hands and walking by the river in the dawn. As far as I know, that was the first night they'd spent together.

I've no idea what the song was, or whether it was ever released — Mick was producing the session."

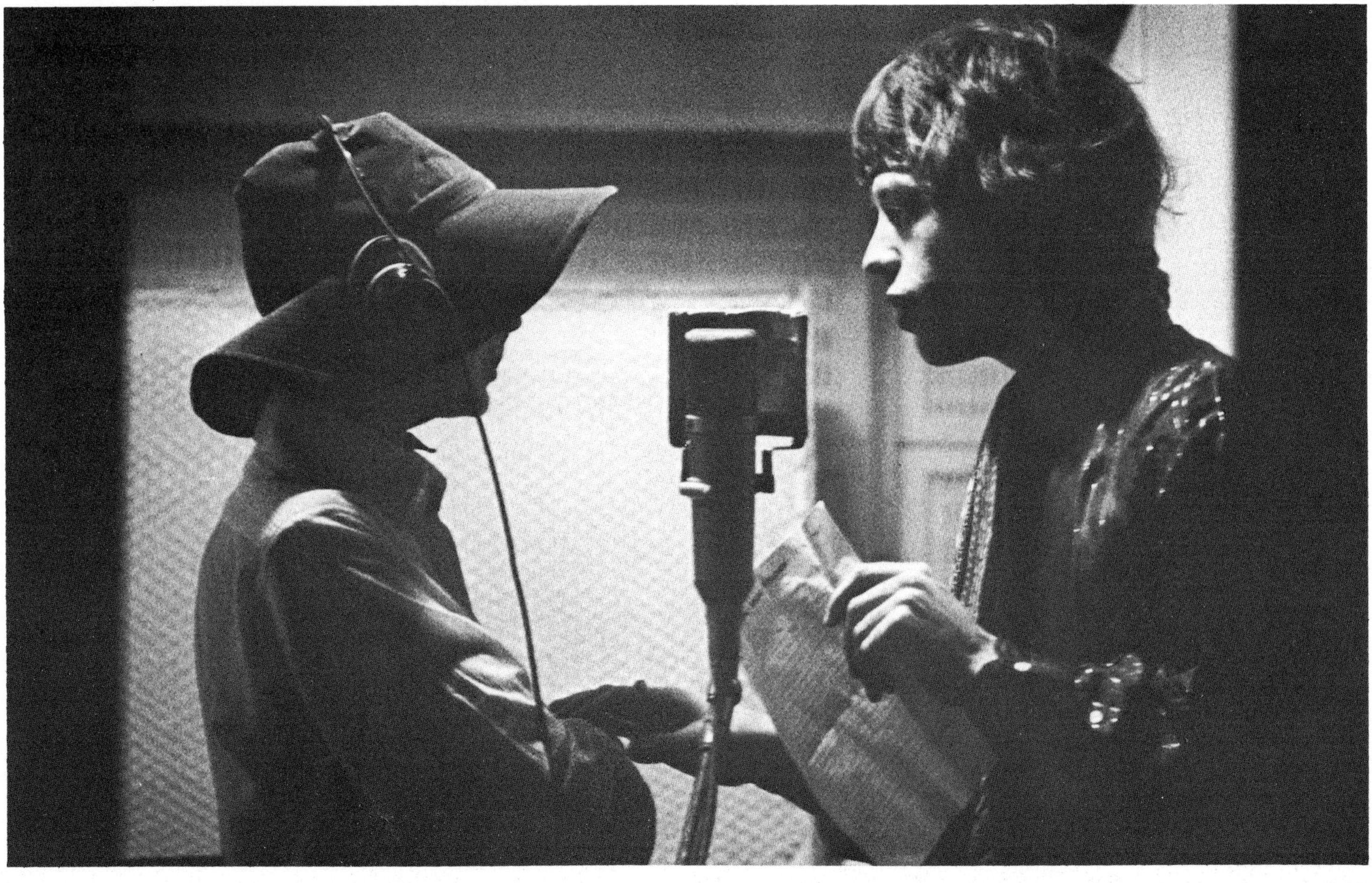

MICK RECORDS MARIANNE, LONDON, 1967

"Mick routining with the backing musicians. The guitarist is John Mark, who accompanied Marianne on concert tours."

Paul McCartney, at the Marianne Faithfull recording session, February: "The same session, another day. In the booth you can see Glyn Johns in the striped shirt, who was co-producing the session, with Mick in the background. McCartney was just sitting in, doing backing vocals."

IN THE STUDIO, LOS ANGELES, 1965

IN THE STUDIO, LOS ANGELES, 1965

RCA Recording Studios, Los Angeles, December 1965
"*Listening to the playback of '19th Nervous Breakdown'. This is pretty weird, as it demonstrates Brian's ability to isolate himself in any situation, and it appears as if the band's attention is focussed on him.*"

"*Wheeling and dealing — business as usual.*"

IN THE STUDIO, LOS ANGELES, 1965

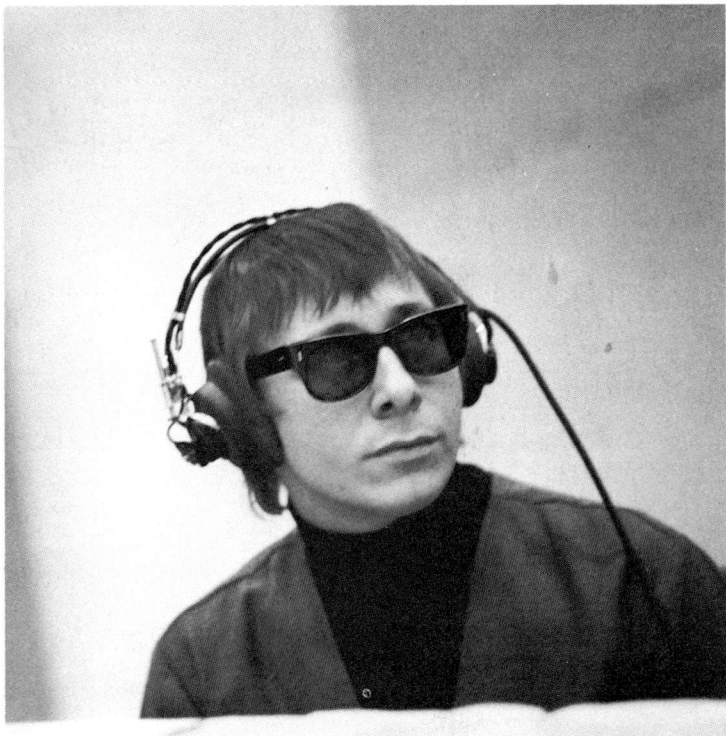

Above: "Jack Nitzsche. A highly talented musician, and very influential on the Stones at the time. His wife would bring cooked meals into the studio for us."

Right: "There were always records lying around. Buying records was an almost continuous process — 'Have you heard this?' — I remember being dragged round Tower records at three in the morning."

Opposite: "Mick's new hat. After the tour had ended, they were able to go out and catch up on fashion."

IN THE STUDIO, LOS ANGELES, 1965

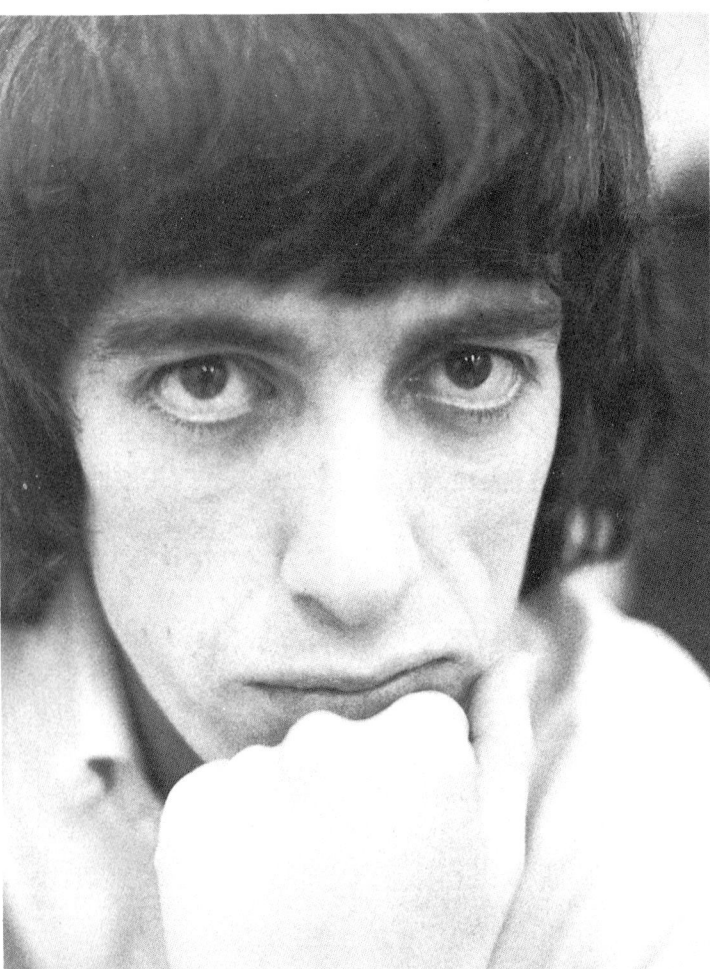

Opposite: "Keith's new image: Byrds-type sunglasses and a motorcycle cop's jacket. If you look back to the photos from the start of the tour, he seems to have aged a hell of a lot."

IN THE STUDIO, LOS ANGELES, 1965

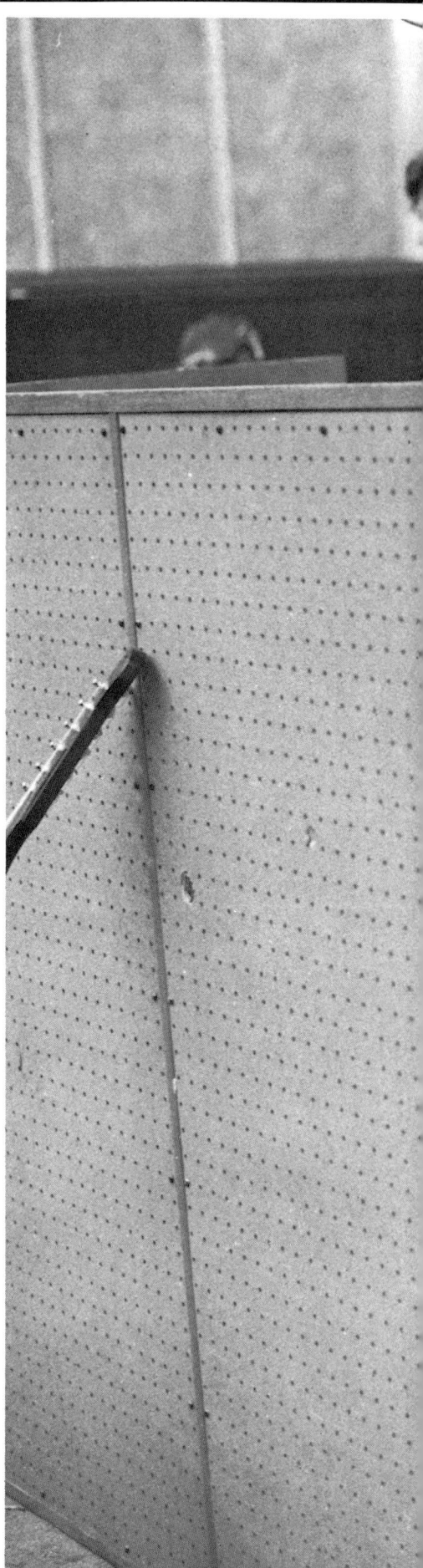

Brian Jones, November 1965. A Florida story: "About half way through the tour, we had a couple of days off in Miami Beach. We were installed in a really flash hotel, and told to just relax...it was a holiday. We spent most of the time laying around on the beach, and discovered these tiny motorboats — basically just a seat and a steering wheel — which could be hired by the hour, and we spent a lot of time messing around on them. Anita Pallenberg had flown in to join Brian, and they spent most of the time in their room...but when Brian emerged, the first thing he wanted to do was have a go on one of these boats. So, he got into one, pointed it out to sea...and kept going. He headed straight out to sea, and just kept going till he ran out of gas. The guy who ran the boat hire had to go after him and tow him back in. Brian thought it was terribly funny and, apart from the fact that we had to pay a huge deposit for hiring boats after that, no harm was done. But if it hadn't been a calm day, he could quite easily have drowned."

IN THE STUDIO, LOS ANGELES, 1965

IN THE STUDIO, LOS ANGELES, 1965

IN THE STUDIO, LOS ANGELES, 1965

Top: "A common habit when listening to playbacks—Andrew biting his nails."

Above: "It was generally accepted that Allen Klein didn't like being photographed, and this is one of the few shots I have of him—enjoying a hamburger during a visit to the studio. He wasn't around on the tour at all, but his presence behind the scenes was felt very strongly. It's amazing, considering his reputation now, but at the time he seemed like 'Uncle Allen', and very much a father figure. Everybody seemed very confident in his business ability; if Andrew was in England, Allen would solve your problems. I think he had a far better idea of the Stones' commercial potential than they did."

IN THE STUDIO, LOS ANGELES, 1965

Right: "Andrew taking the piss out of the contortions photographers (ie myself) undergo in order to take pictures."

Far right: "A fairly rare shot of Brian and Andrew in conversation. Not that they didn't talk, but you didn't see them together like this very often."

Right: "Brian's famous cock-a-doodle-doo impression. Along with various varieties of Nanker, Brian would pull this whenever he noticed a camera on him."

Far right: "Mick and Andrew with Dave Hassinger, the engineer, discussing the playback."

Right: "The Dirty Old Man Of The Rolling Stones. Bill makes a lewd suggestion."

Far right: "Keith listening to playbacks, a copy of 'Guns Of The Old West' at the ready — this was just a few days after our 'cowboy' trip to Phoenix. The mixing desk looks incredibly primitive now, but it was state-of-the-art technology then — Presley used to record in this studio."

Between The Buttons cover session, Primrose Hill, November 1966: "The first roll of film I took that morning — this was taken very early in the morning, after an all night recording session at Olympic Studios in Barnes. I really wanted to do an organised session with them, and the only way we could do it was to 'kidnap' the band after they'd finished recording. We piled them into Andrew's Rolls and headed for Primrose Hill in North London, which would provide a lot of sky for the background and was convenient for where everybody was living. We got there at about six in the morning, and started walking up the hill, when we heard this flute music. When we reached the top of the hill, it turned out to be this well known London character called Moxie, who was sort of a prototype hippie — just standing on his own playing the flute. Mick walked up to him and offered him a joint, and his only response — to the joint, and to the sight of the Rolling Stones wandering around on a hilltop at dawn — was, 'Ah! Breakfast!'

"I used a home-made filter to get the misty effect — a piece of glass held in front of the lens and (in this case) smeared with vaseline. The band took the piss out of me for using this Mickey Mouse contraption, but Andrew had confidence in what I was doing. I took a lot of pictures in a short space of time, because everybody started to feel the cold pretty quickly. As you can see, Brian was a pain in the arse — he didn't want to be there at all. But however obstructive he was, it just reinforced his image, so it didn't really matter. In frames 10, 11 and 12 you can clearly see the buttons on Charlie's stylish jacket that gave the album it's title."

JUMPING JACK FLASH, 1967

Mick Jagger, Harley House, October 1967: *"Portraits of Mick, taken at his flat, for a magazine. My relationship with the Stones as a whole was pretty much over by this time, but I still saw Mick, Keith and Charlie around for a while, and Mick was always very friendly with me. The close-up was taken with a wide-angle lens, so that he would really jump out at you — very molesting."*

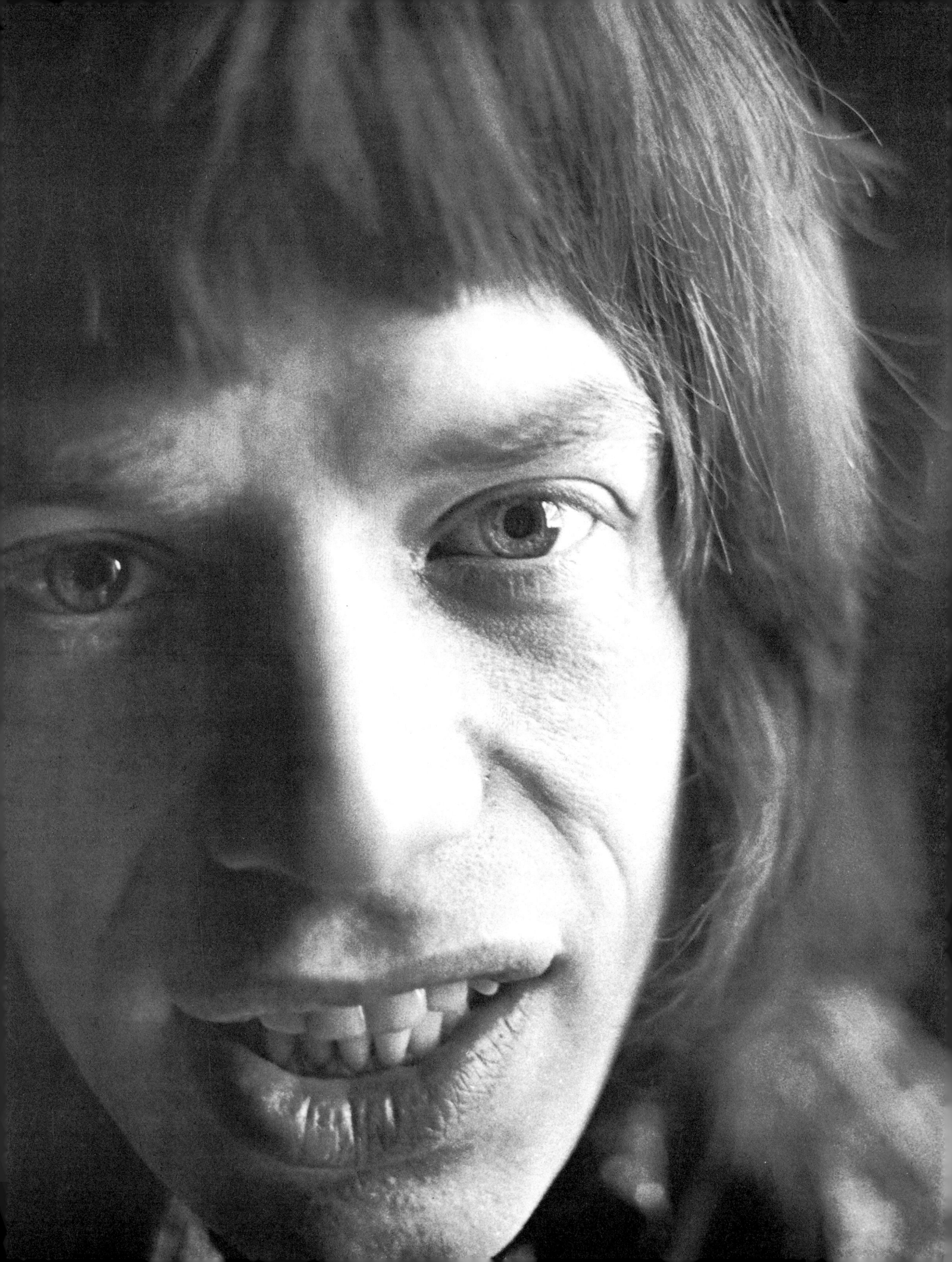

RUBY TUESDAY NIGHTS, 1966

RUBY TUESDAY NIGHTS, 1966

Recording sessions, Olympic Studios, November 1966:
"The photos here, and on pages 96, 97, 98 and 99, were taken using a masking technique of my own devising, which gives them an ethereal, psychedelic quality."

RUBY TUESDAY NIGHTS, 1966

"I wanted to get away from the usual, boring studio portraits, while still using available light—the Stones didn't like flash, apart from anything else. None of the photographs were posed — the band were recording all the time."

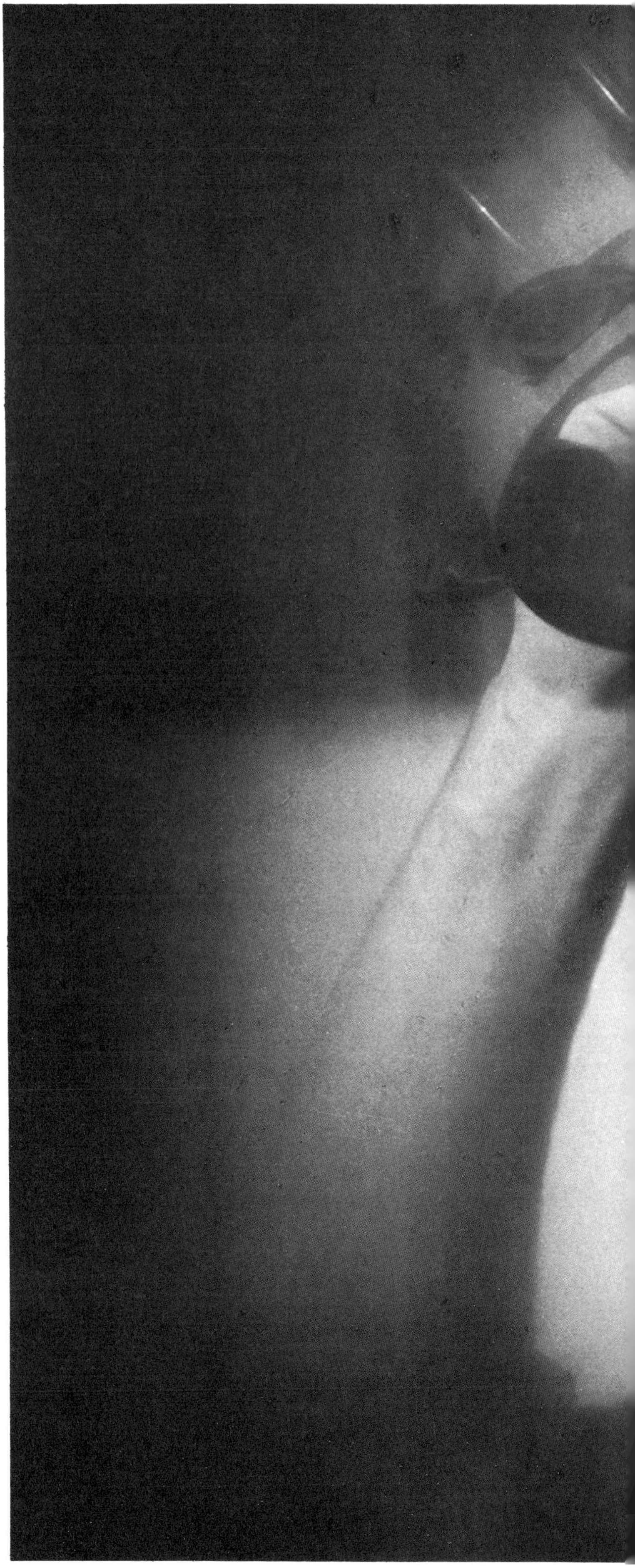

RUBY TUESDAY NIGHTS, 1966

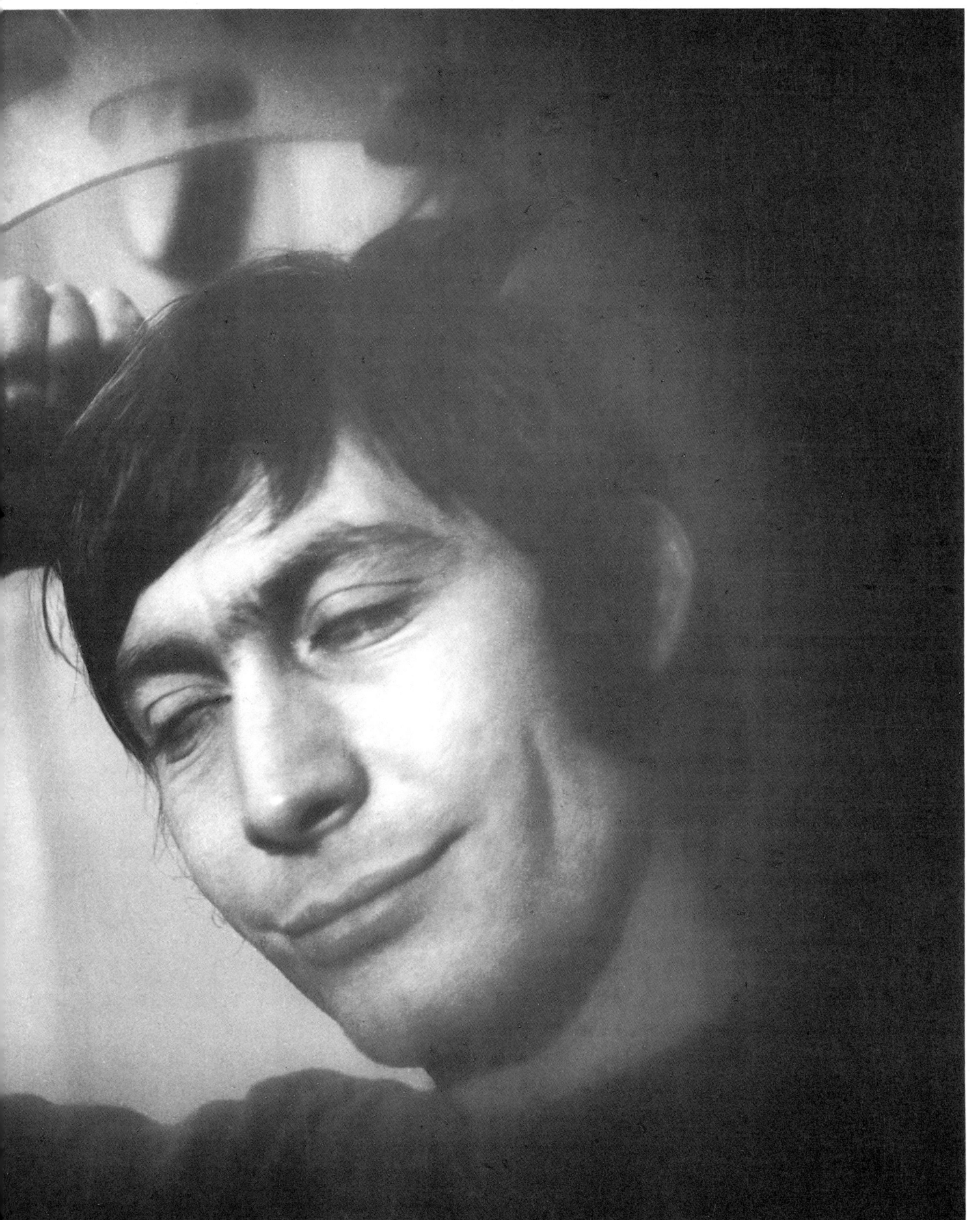

RUBY TUESDAY NIGHTS, 1966

RUBY TUESDAY NIGHTS, 1966

"Bill's missing...because he was missing.. Everybody knew what the Stones looked like, so I was trying to make things more abstract. It worked, as far as we were concerned, and it doesn't look dated even now."

THEIR SATANIC MAJESTIES, 1967

THEIR SATANIC MAJESTIES, 1967

The 'Satanic Majesties' sessions, August 1967: "A very difficult and tense time. Brian was in a hell of a state, and the rest weren't much better. They weren't properly rehearsed, and didn't even really have any finished songs. There were tremendous undercurrents of intrigue going on, and it was quite clear that things were going from bad to worse between Andrew and the band. As it was Andrew that had asked me to photograph the sessions, my position was uncomfortable, to say the least. The atmosphere was so bad that it was almost impossible to get any decent material. In the end, I just left."

NOT FADE AWAY LONDON, 1982

"I didn't see the Stones again for fifteen years. In May, 1982 they were rehearsing for their British tour at Shepperton Studios and the *Observer* magazine, who were doing a piece on the band, thought it would be great if I did the pictures, because of my earlier association with them. Apparently the Stones' office thought so too, and we began to try to set up a session. We went through a lot of false starts and red herrings, the excuse being that the Stones were under a lot of pressure with rehearsals, and very short of time. A day was finally agreed on, and the session was set up for midnight, which was when they started rehearsing. That day I got a whole lot of extraordinary phonecalls from the Stones' office...'Mick's just got up, and he's in the bath — we'll call you right back', then half an hour later...'Mick's still in the bath, but Keith's up now, and says he's looking forward to seeing you', then an hour later...'Mick's out of the bath now, he says it's definitely on for tonight, so we'll call again in an hour and tell you where'. Eventually I got a call about 10 o'clock, telling me to go to the Stones' office in Cheyne Walk immediately, so my assistant and I drove over there, met the Stones' people, and followed them to Shepperton.

"When we got there, we were guided passed the security people to a huge sound stage with equipment set up in it...and there were the Stones. Keith and I embraced, and went through an 'amazing to see you' routine. One of the first things he said was 'Do you remember Phoenix?' I was really surprised, and touched, that he should have remembered it after all he's been through, and it was very important to me...just because of friendship. Mick was really friendly, Bill acted as if it had only been a matter of days since we'd last met; Charlie was a bit cool, funnily enough. Ronnie Wood was quite sweet — 'I'm the one you never photographed'.

"Mick said 'You doing this for the *Observer*? Well, don't use flash man, don't use flash...there's enough light for you here, ain't there?

You can do it, you can do anything with a camera, Gerard'.... It really was like slipping back fifteen years. I said 'OK, but I want to do something for the magazine cover, so maybe we could do a set-up piece'. 'We're really pushed for time man'. So I said, 'Well, I could set something up in another room, and you needn't be bothered — when you break for a meal, just come in for ten minutes and we'll shoot it then'. 'OK, but not tonight. Come back and do it another night...just shoot reportage now'. So I shot all night, 'till about 5.30 in the morning — the music was great, and the whole thing was wonderful. Toby, my young assistant just couldn't believe it, that I really *had* been that close to the band...nor could the people in the Stones' camp — they were all amazed by the reactions of Mick and Keith, and they asked me that night if I'd like to be the tour photographer. Shirley Watts was there, and Marlon Richards, and Keith's dad, who he'd literally rediscovered only weeks before. They whole thing was like a family reunion, and when they played 'Satisfaction' and 'Get Off My Cloud', it was real throwback time...for me, anyway. I arranged to go back two or three nights later to do a set-piece in one of the side room for the *Observer* cover, and drove home about six in the morning, on a real high from it all. I couldn't help thinking that if this worked well, I might get a chance to do another album sleeve for them. At the time I was thinking of phasing out or rock photography, and that would have been a great thing to finish with: full circle, ending where I'd really begun.

"I turned up a couple of nights later, as arranged, with *all* my equipment, but the moment I walked in, the atmosphere was very

strange. Only Charlie and Keith were there, and Keith said 'Ah, you're back again'. I said, 'Yeah, we're going to do this session', and he said 'I don't think we are'. I asked why, and he said 'Well, you remind us of really bad times. Whenever we look at you we think of 1·5 million dollars'. I assumed he meant the money owed them by Klein, or whoever, and I just said 'Well, that was nothing to do with me', and Keith said 'Yeah...but you're the only one who's around', and turned away.

"I was really shocked. I briefed my assistant that there was something weird going on, and decided that I might as well hang around until they threw me out, just in case I got some extra material. Word came through that Bill was ill and wasn't coming; then Alan Edwards, the Stones' PR man, asked me if I'd take some black & white shots of Mick and Keith for the press — they'd pay me if I gave them the film. I told him I'd have to use flash, and he said he'd ask Mick about it. Mick finally arrived about 3.30, really drunk and aggressive — he had that blinkered, 'don't fuck with me' expression of his, pacing up and down. Edwards asked him about doing some pictures, and he said 'Yeah, alright, let's do it. Don't take too long about it'. So I did some black & white shots, gave the film to them and left.

"Driving back, Toby was really shocked by what had happened. I just said '*That's* why I don't want to deal with this any more'...you just can't relate to that level of schizophrenia. It was very bizarre — my whole relationship with the Stones had been re-enacted in the course of two nights. The black & white pictures appeared in the *Star*...I stuck my bill in, and thought 'fuck that'." *Gered Mankowitz, London, 1984.*